W9-ATE-449

DEC 1981

RECEIVED

OHIO DOMINICAN
COLLEGE LIBRARY
COLUMBUS, OHIO
43219

A
Matter
of
Time

JF Schotter
Schotter, Roni.
A matter of time

A Matter of Time

Roni Schotter

COLLINS
New York and Cleveland

J
S

Acknowledgments:
Portion of "I Knew a Woman" from The Collected Poems of
Theodore Roethke reprinted by permission of Doubleday and
Co., Inc. and Faber and Faber Publishers, Ltd.
Portion of "Fruit Gathering" from Collected Poems And Plays
by Rabindranath Tagore: Copyright 1916 by Macmillan
Publishing Co., Inc., renewed 1944 by Rabindranath Tagore
reprinted by permission of Macmillan Publishing Co., Inc.
and Macmillan Press, Ltd.

Library of Congress Cataloging in Publication Data

Schotter, Roni.   A matter of time.

SUMMARY: A 16-year-old girl develops her sense of self
while coping with the grief over her mother's death.

[1. Death—Fiction. 2. Identity—Fiction]
I. Title.
PZ7.S3765Mat   [Fic]   79-12351
ISBN 0-529-05510-4

Published by William Collins Publishers, Inc.
New York and Cleveland, 1979.

Copyright © 1979 by Roni Schotter
All rights reserved
PRINTED IN THE UNITED STATES OF AMERICA

4

For my mother,
Edna Agines Goldberg

"I knew a woman lovely in her bones"

5

115290

*The characters and situations
in this book are
fictional ideas and
are not meant to
portray actual persons or events.*

Every once in a while I get an urge to visit my mother. It comes on suddenly and is sort of a lumpy, choking feeling in my throat. Before I know what's happening, I turn to my father, who's usually washing dishes, and say, "Going out. Back in an hour." He always mumbles something under his breath about how I'm never home, as I race out the door.

The first time I visited my mom, I kept my distance. It seemed so strange and a little silly. I said a few words about loving her, cried a bit, and was gone in about four minutes flat. I felt like a coward, but after all, she didn't know. Or did she . . . ?

Since then, I've visited her a few other times—whenever that lumpy feeling comes into my throat. Each time, it gets a little easier. When the grass started to grow in, I started to feel more at ease. I like to kneel on the spot and slide my fingers through the bright new blades. It feels a little like I'm touching her.

Once I lay down on the grass to see how I'd fit. On my back, with my arms close to my sides and my legs extended, I could watch the clouds move lazily across the sky. Of course I fit perfectly, with room to spare, which me made me feel good on the one hand and spooked on the other. What did it feel like to be *underneath*? I guess I looked pretty strange to anyone passing by, but then the nice thing about a cemetery is that it's what my mom used to call "a fine and private place." You can do your own thing—unless one of the gardeners drives by or a whole cortège of mourners passes through. But then, it's my property—the only place that's really mine. Some people own houses or woods or farms. I own a grave.

Everywhere you look there are stone monuments. Some are huge private buildings surrounded by trees and hills and decorated with ornate sculptures. The humbler ones just stick up out of the ground in rows with short sayings on them. Some have simple crosses, Jewish stars, or tiny American flags.

Our plot is located in the flat section. We chose the place because we didn't have much money. My dad was out of work again, the hospital wanted to be paid, and anyway it didn't seem to matter that much. They showed us a dried-out spot where the sun had grilled everything a dull brown. Two roads met in a place with no trees. We had a choice of there or to the right of it by about three feet. It's amazing how little space it takes to bury someone.

My dad chose the spot nearest the road. He looked down at his feet and mumbled something like, "That's that, I guess." My mother was in the

8

hospital then, technically still alive, so the business of choosing a grave seemed a little ghoulish.

When I showed up recently to see the tombstone that had been laid, I was disappointed. It measures about one foot square and lies flat on the ground. You can hardly see it. Because there's no room for long speeches like "Beloved Mother," "Wife," etc., my older sister Jane and her husband Jim had only one word engraved on the stone, *Shantih*. It's a Hindu word that means something about everlasting peace. They got it out of a long poem by T. S. Eliot.

It's been almost two months since my mom died, and I haven't read much T. S. Eliot or much of anything in that time. But I sure have done a lot of thinking. About death. About life. All kinds of things. I guess I always thought my mom would live forever. Or at least as long as I lived. Sometimes I'm amazed that only eight months ago I was such a child. Eight months ago—I've done a lot of growing up since then.

It was back in January that I first discovered my mother was sick. For several weeks she'd been gulping aspirin and sucking hard candies, trying to get rid of an annoying sore throat. She didn't stay in bed or anything. My mom wasn't like that. Except for the candy wrappers she left in a trail around the house, you would never have guessed she wasn't feeling well.

But one day when I came home early from a senior class meeting at school, I was surprised to find my mom, paintbrush in hand, hard at work at her easel.

"Didn't you teach today?" I asked.

"Nope. Went to the doctor," she said, adding a streak of blue to her painting and then standing back to peer at it from the distance. "He says I have to go into the hospital. Damn! I have classes, meetings, and the deadline for the art show. Now I won't have time to finish anything."

"The hospital?" I gasped, ignoring her complaints. "But why?"

"This stupid sore throat. I should never have gone for a checkup. They found a tumor on my lung, and now they insist on removing it."

"A tumor?" My heart was pounding in my head. "You haven't got . . . cancer?"

"Oh, Lisl honey," she said, putting down her paintbrush and taking my chin in her hand. "Don't be silly. Would I be standing here talking to you like this if I thought I had cancer? The thing's benign. They're sure of it."

"Then why remove it?" I asked, still suspicious.

"Because that's how doctors make money. On stupid women like me who are foolish enough to go to them. Look," she said, picking up her paint-

10

brush again, "forget about it and be a sweetheart. Make dinner tonight so I can get on with this painting?"

"Okay," I said.

"And do me one other favor? Go out and get me a paper? I forgot to buy one today."

"Sure," I said, feeling relieved. It was silly to worry. My mom wasn't worried. And she certainly didn't sound terribly ill. In fact, she was her usual busy and demanding self.

For the next couple of weeks I went about my business—school, exams, and other annoyances—while my mom went about hers. She was as busy as ever, taking only a minute here and there to swallow a teaspoon of honey for her throat.

The day of the operation finally arrived. It was scheduled for early Sunday morning. My mom insisted that I spend Saturday night and Sunday at my best friend Jo's house while she was in surgery. "You can visit me on Sunday night when it's all over," she instructed. "But do me a favor and bring me a few books to read. Otherwise I'll die of boredom."

"Sure," I promised.

Early Saturday morning my parents left for the hospital in the "family" car, and I jumped on my creaky old bike and pedaled off to Jo's. My dad and I had arranged to meet at home Sunday afternoon, eat dinner, and return together to the hospital to visit my mom.

11

Jo and I spent all day Saturday doing homework and all day Sunday locked in a movie theater watching a double feature of *Horse Feathers* and *Duck Soup*. Between the two of us, we must have broken the world's record for movie munching—we finished off three huge boxes of buttered popcorn, two candy bars, and three Cokes. As long as Groucho was making wisecracks, I felt fine, but whenever Harpo got serious and played his harp, I found myself wondering how my mom was doing.

It was almost five o'clock when I finally coasted into our driveway. I was late, and I was sure my father would be impatiently awaiting me. I had bicycled the whole distance from the movie theater in just under fifteen minutes. My cheeks burned from the icy winter breeze, and my breath hung in front of my face like a heavy gray balloon. I could hardly wait to get inside the warm house. I dug deep into my jacket pocket, pulled out my key, and tried to maneuver it into the back-door lock. My fingers were so cold and stiff they barely worked. I finally inserted the key, twisted it, and pushed open the door.

The house was silent and dark. "Dad . . . You home?" I yelled. There was no sound. Only the pines scratched an answer against the kitchen window. Maybe he's stuck in traffic, I thought. On Sunday? I shrugged my shoulders and flicked on a light. I was just about to take off my jacket and start dinner when the phone rang. It was my father.

"Hello," he said, sounding upset. "Everything will be all right."

"But, Dad, why shouldn't it be?" There was a long silence. "Weren't you supposed to meet me at home?" I asked, feeling confused.

"Look," he said grudgingly. "I'll let you speak to Jane or Jim."

"Jane? Jim? What are *they* doing here? I thought they were in the city."

My father didn't answer. There was some mumbling in the background, and then Jane's voice crackled breathlessly on the phone. "Something's happened."

"What? What's happened?" I pleaded.

"Something. . . . Come to the hospital. Sixth floor."

"But what's happened?" I screamed in frustration.

There was no response. Jane had already hung up.

For a moment I stood motionless in the middle of the kitchen. Then I slammed down the receiver and dashed out of the house, my mind a madhouse of images. Medics, stretchers, bedpans, and nurses whirled crazily about. Something had happened. But what? I thought about Jane. She was really a bum. All the way up from New York, and she hadn't even told me what was going on. What was

13

she doing at the hospital anyway? I was furious and scared at the same time.

I caught a bus, and in fifteen minutes I was in the hospital, running through the long, green corridors, weaving this way and that, wondering if I'd ever get there. Just when I thought I'd never make it, I saw Jane, Jim, and my father pacing or rather circling around and around and back and forth outside a huge room filled with all kinds of weird electronic equipment, racing nurses, and hushed tones. The three of them looked really odd.

Jim smiled briefly at me. "Want to see her?"

"Of course," I answered, puzzled by such a senseless question. For several seconds he looked at me. Then he pulled me toward him and held me in his arms.

I felt a little strange. I'd only recently stopped feeling shy with Jim. After all, he's a guy, and watching him snuggle up to my sister whenever they think someone isn't looking makes me feel all sorts of sexy feelings in my body. To tell the truth, I used to have a crush on him. He's tall and thin and strong-looking with smooth sandy-colored hair. He dresses conservatively—crew necks, pressed jeans, even a tweed jacket. There's something solid and comforting about the serious but kind expression you usually see on his face.

He and Jane are a perfect match. Not that they look alike. They don't. She's short and dark and not nearly so together-looking. But they're both in love with words. She's a book editor, and he's an English professor. Jane loves to talk, and Jim loves to listen. They love each other an awful lot, and I think that's nice, but though I'd never admit it out loud, I used to wish Jim felt that way about me.

When I got over my shyness, I learned how to talk to Jim—straight. That was a relief. Jane is usually too busy playing older sister to listen to anything I have to say, and my father never seems all that interested. I like having Jim around. Like an older brother, he makes me feel secure.

I pulled myself away from him, he took me by the arm, and we entered the room. The sharp smell of alcohol burned the inside of my nose. Suddenly I felt a tingling sensation in my fingertips. Nerves, I guessed. We passed in front of a bed and I slowed down, but Jim tugged on my arm to pull me in another direction. How could he tell who was who? We passed three or four more beds, and finally he stopped me. There was this thing—it looked sort of like a robot—wires and tubes going in and out, a strange plastic mask over a pinkish face, glaring white sheets, and a hint of wavy black hair. I was frozen to the spot. That was my mom, and worse, she was awake in this really strange way.

All I could think of was, Smile, so I smiled and moved toward her. "How are you feeling?" I asked stupidly. Of course she couldn't answer. I tried to touch her, but with all the wiring and tubes I couldn't find her hands, so all I could do was to run my pinky across a narrow spot on her forehead where the oxygen mask ended. Her skin felt moist and steamy. Through the mask I could see that she smiled in a vague way and then closed her eyes. There was nothing to say. Jim gave me a pull, and we hurried out of the room.

It was awful, but at least the surgery was over, and soon she'd be well. But something confused me. Outside the big room, Jane and my dad were clutching one another. My father isn't exactly the demonstrative type. Oh, he has feelings, all right. But he usually hides them so well, it's hard to remember that they're there. The last time I saw him touch anyone was at Jane's wedding, when he got a little drunk and hugged her like a proud parent. So what was going on? What was happening?

I looked from face to face, and all I saw was despair and helplessness. Suddenly I knew, and I was furious. Furious at the world and the dumb scurrying nurses and the useless doctors with their measured important steps and most of all at the gruesome threesome who were too cowardly to speak to me.

"She's going to die, isn't she?" I rasped, and the words slashed deep into my throat. Silence. "She's going to die, isn't she?" I managed again. My father's face turned the same colorless gray as his hair, and out of his mouth came a terrible sobbing sound that he tried to muffle with the back of his hand.

The sound tore at me and made me gasp. It was the first time I'd ever seen my father lose control of himself. Whenever Jane and I had a fight, my mom would get terribly upset. But my father would just quietly leave the room. When my mom accused him of not helping us work things out, his face would become tight and red. It looked as if his head might explode with all the anger it contained, but it never did. He always remained silent. But now he was sobbing and moaning. Even his hand couldn't muffle the sound

Jim grabbed him, and Jane grabbed me. And then I heard Jane's voice. "They thought it was only a small tumor, benign, but when they opened her up to remove it, they discovered it was too late. The cancer had already spread through her lungs. There wasn't anything they could do but close her up again. It's terminal and only a matter of time. She doesn't know yet. No one's told her. She's too weak."

My father made that strange sound again, and I felt dizzy and far away. Tiny specks of light danced across the green walls. Then everything began to grow dark and close and warm. I sank to the floor and put my head between my knees. In a second my family was around me.

17

"Lisl," I heard my father call. It sounded like the wind whistling through trees far away. "Are you all right?"

Slowly I raised my head, pulled myself together, and tried to sound tough, "A-okay. How long has she got?"

Again, silence. My father looked like himself again. He had his "too-many-questions" look on. Jim whispered, "Still some time, but first she has to recover from the operation. That will take a while, and then maybe some more time. We haven't really asked yet."

"Recover?" I nearly screamed. "Recover for what, so that she can die? Why not leave her alone and let her die now?" My father glared at me, turned his back, and walked away. "But, Jim, Jim . . . why does she have to get better in order to die?" I pleaded.

Jim looked miserable. "Because that's the way it is. The cancer isn't strong enough to kill her yet, so she'll recover, go home, and then eventually it will get stronger and kill her."

I felt dizzy again. I didn't believe him. I *couldn't* believe him. I felt so helpless. What was this thing called cancer? A monster? Well, then I would kill it. Or wound it and slow it down. I couldn't understand something invisible that was so strong—strong enough to kill my mother. It made no sense to me. I decided that as soon as I

18

could find a doctor who could tell me how much time we had, I'd figure something out. I hated my family for not fighting. They had given up without a struggle. Not me! I yanked myself away from Jim and started running.

"Lisl!" Jim called. But I couldn't stop to answer. I just ran and ran. Back along the snakelike corridors of the ugly green hospital. Running. Running as fast as I could. Running away. Sweating. Panting. Gasping for breath. Then, slowing down. Over my shoulder I could see that my family was out of sight. Some nurses wearing starched white uniforms and starched white faces were staring at me. I had reached the elevators. The heavy doors parted, and I pushed in. I was the shortest person in the elevator. High above my head, everyone chatted and tittered as if they were guests in a fancy hotel.

"Her room looks like a florist's shop. *She's* certainly going to be fixed for plants when she gets home."

"Meet you in the coffeeshop at the break?"

"Sure. Catch you then."

I shoved my way out of the elevator into the lobby, spotted the phone booths, and ran to the telephone books. "Travis, Trayman, Traynor . . . Traynor, Herman, M.D. . . . 672-4300. 672-4300, 672-4300," I repeated over and over in my head. I reached in my pocket for a dime, found a quarter and pushed it in. Clink. Clank. Clunk. Pause. My hands were shaking and sweating. The receiver was damp where I grasped it. The phone rang.

"Dr. Traynor's office. Ms. Gordon speaking."

"It's Lisl Gilbert. I want to talk to Dr. Traynor."

"Oh . . . your mother. . . . Let me see if I can get the doctor." (How did *she* know?)

I waited for what felt like hours. I was panting. Panting, trembling, and perspiring. I couldn't seem to control my body any more.

"Lisl," a deep voice said into the phone. "You're the little one."

"Yes," I managed. "That's me."

"I'm terribly sorry about all of this. It's an awful shock. Is there anything I can do for you?"

Do? A voice inside me screamed. Sure. Make her well, you idiot. Isn't that your job? "She's going to die, isn't she?" I whispered softly.

"Yes."

"There's . . . nothing you can do?"

"Nothing anyone can do. Only ease her pain. If it's any consolation, you know I—all of us—will do the best we know how."

"Dr. Traynor," I gulped. "H-h-how long?"

"I wish I could tell you. It's very hard with cancer. We never know."

"A year?"

"No."

"A month?" I sobbed, almost pleading.

20

"Probably a few months. Maybe a bit longer. There's still time, you know. A little. I wish I could tell you something better. But I guess you want the truth."

"Sure," I said stiffly. "And thanks."

"Lisl," the voice added, "take care of yourself."

"Sure." I hung up the phone. My stomach had started to heave, and I was sobbing. I yanked at the handle on the glass door, and burst out of the booth like a small explosion. Straight into someone's big arms. It was Jim.

"Jim—" I cried. "Why?"

"There's no reason," he said quietly.

"But how did it happen?"

"We don't know."

"But you did. You did! You *all* did. You *must* have! Or you wouldn't all be here. You kept it from me. All of you. You kept it from me," I screamed. My hand tightened into a fist, and I started punching Jim. Hard. And slapping him. Till it stung. Trying to make him hurt the way I did inside. "Why didn't you tell me? Why? Why?"

Jim grabbed me by the wrists and pulled me back into his arms. "We didn't know, Lisl. Honestly, we didn't. We thought it was something small. It was supposed to be benign. But when they told your Dad how bad it was, he was frightened and he called us. We raced up here and . . . well, we didn't want to upset you—"

"Because I'm 'the little one.' " I interrupted.

21

Jim looked embarrassed. "I'm sorry, Lisl. Really sorry. For not respecting you and for what you and all of us have to face now." He looked tired and lost. Like a sad child. Suddenly I felt sorry for him. He wasn't all that old himself.

"Forget it," I said. "We all make mistakes." I slipped my arm through his, and together we walked across the room to a long couch where Jane and my father were sitting.

"Are you all right, Lisl?" Jane asked. Her face was wet with tears. I nodded. My father sat slumped on the couch, mumbling incoherently to himself. Gray hair fell forward over his eyes, keeping his face in shadow.

"Dad," I said patiently, "You should have called me at Jo's when you found out."

He swallowed hard and tugged at his shirt collar. Then he lifted his head and looked at me. "I couldn't, Lisl, I couldn't. I'm sorry."

"It's okay," I said, taking his hand. "I guess you didn't realize that I. . . ." My father wasn't listening. He was mumbling again.

"I begged her to go. I begged her to go," he said over and over.

"Go where?" I asked.

"To the doctor!" he shouted angrily. "But she was too busy—too busy. For weeks, she was too busy to think about herself or a sore throat. I begged her. Then it was too late. Too late," he said, and he sucked in his lower lip and bit down on it.

He wasn't accustomed to talking about his feelings, and now he seemed to be trying to swallow back his words.

We walked to the car and slowly drove home. Busy, I thought. My father's words buzzed in my head. In art class when I was six years old, I made a painting of my mother. I painted bright red lips, big dark eyes, wavy black hair, and the prettiest face I could manage. I pasted a veil over the face (in those days well-dressed women wore veils) and lettered BUZY BUZY, O SO BUZY! The art teacher was so excited by my creation that she telephoned my mother to tell her about her talented daughter.

When my mom showed up to take me home, she stared first at the painting and then at me for a long time. Her face looked worried and sad. She thanked my art teacher and said my painting was "significant"—a mysterious-sounding word that I didn't understand. She and my teacher shook hands, and I felt myself being hurried out of the room.

In the street, my mom squatted down until I could look right into her pretty dark eyes. She asked me if I'd like to go to the zoo. Back then, I loved polar bears. The mere thought of them sent me into a frenzy of excitement. I jumped up and down, hugged my mother, and yelled so loud that I almost didn't hear her explaining that we'd have to go another day because she had something important to do. I looked down at my thick brown lace-up shoes. I thought about the word "significant" and the word "important" and tried to figure out what they meant and why I didn't like them. Suddenly I felt my mother draw me to her and kiss me. "Never mind," she said quietly, "we'll go this afternoon."

It was a wonderful day. We walked together and gobbled Cracker Jacks and peanuts and even got to see the polar bears being fed. My mother lifted me up and sat me on the railing and I watched a polar bear dive into the water and then climb out and shake himself dry. It was one of the best days I'd ever spent.

After that, I figured all I had to do to get my mother to take me to the zoo was to paint another picture of her. But the next time I showed my mom a picture of herself, she looked concerned. "Lisl," she said, "you must learn to be original. Each time you do something, it must be special. Don't be content to do the same old thing all the time. *Be special.*" Then she patted me on the head and went off to a meeting.

That's the way it always was with my mom. She never seemed to have much time for me. She was always busy running from one meeting or activity to the next. She was a living example of her own advice. She was both original and special. When she wasn't going to an exercise class or a discussion group, she was teaching art history or painting or reading some great book. Long before

24

it was fashionable, she was eating health foods and baking organic breads. By the time I entered high school, I'd pretty much learned how to take care of myself. But I'd never learned how to be original or special the way my mother was.

Being around my mom, who was still as pretty as she was when I was six, didn't make things very easy for me. The strange thing was that no matter how busy she was, my mother always seemed to have time to be present whenever one of my dates would appear. The bell would ring while I was upstairs frantically trying to cover my pimpled face with make-up.

"Not ready yet," I'd call. "Tell him I'll be down in a minute."

"Take your time," my mother would answer as she walked to the front door in some long elegant dress. She'd open the door, the thick scent of fragrance floating mysteriously around her. From upstairs I could hear my stunned date stammering, "Are y-y-you Mrs. Gilbert?"

"Certainly," she'd answer. "Come on in."

I'd appear at the top of the stairs and clear my throat, but my date was usually too involved to notice. He'd be following my mother into the living room, oblivious to the fact that I was trying to make a graceful, relaxed entrance down the stairs. I usually found him, whoever he was, engrossed in an appreciative discussion of my mother's paintings, which covered the walls of our home.

One day, after I had decided to stop going out with good old Bruce Bomes, I came home late from school to find him hunched over a cup of papaya mint tea staring adoringly at my mother. She sat cross-legged on the sofa in beige pants and tunic, explaining her exercise classes and how she was learning deep breathing and self-hypnosis. Sitting at her feet, Bruce Bomes looked like her devoted disciple. I cleared my throat, and Bruce Bomes nodded at me looking as if *he'd* been hypnotized.

"Hello, come and join us," my mom invited.

"No, thanks," I said curtly. Something made me feel as if I didn't belong there. I certainly didn't feel dressed for it—old pants and a borrowed sweater from a friend. I climbed the stairs with wafts of perfume spiraling up after me and a funny, nauseous feeling in my stomach. From up in my room I could hear the murmur of voices talking about me. I don't know why, but I felt jealous. Jealous and confused.

"Lisl," my mother said.

"Lisl," the voice became louder. I looked up and saw Jane standing outside the car in the darkness. I don't know how long I'd been sitting in the back seat daydreaming. Jim and my father had already entered the house and were turning on the lights. "Lisl," Jane repeated. "You're really out

26

of it. Aren't you going to come inside? We're home."

"Oh yeah . . . sure," I said, coming to. "Well, actually . . . maybe I'll just sit here a while and think."

"You sure you're all right?" Jane asked. Her face was swollen from crying, but she still looked pretty—like my mother.

"Yeah, I'm okay."

Jane shrugged and walked toward the house, her short dark hair bouncing up and down with every step. I watched her disappear.

Except for this terrible day, Jane seemed happier now than I'd ever known her, ever since she'd married Jim and moved to New York. She was more on her own, I guessed. But every once in a while when she and Jim came to visit, she looked the way she had in the old days.

Jim and my mom liked to have long literary discussions. Whenever they did, Jane looked like someone who was suffocating and needed air. She'd break up the discussion with a nervous giggle and the suggestion that we all go to a movie. I never asked Jane about how she felt. We didn't talk much, but I suspected that when she was around my mom, she felt a little uncomfortable, sort of the way I did when my mom and Bruce Bomes were together. Well, I realized, Jane and I would never have to feel uncomfortable again. My mom wouldn't be talking to Jim or Bruce Bomes or

27

anyone any more. We'd never have that problem to worry about again. Never. Never was such a big word. It meant forever. It seemed melodramatic. Wasn't my mom really inside the house? Wasn't she, this very minute, talking to Jim about a book? It seemed impossible to believe that she was in a hospital room dying of cancer. I knew she was in the house preparing a late supper. I climbed out of the car into the darkness, slammed the door shut, and headed toward the house. My mother was probably wondering what I'd been doing out there in the dark all alone.

Early the next morning, I left for school. Jim and Jane were driving back to New York, and my father had already gone to the hospital. It was a sunny day and I had plenty of time, so instead of taking the bus, I decided to walk to school. Halfway there I heard the sound of a motorbike approaching. It was my friend Jeff. "How's your mother?" he called. "I heard she was in the hospital. She's okay, isn't she?" he asked shyly, jumping off the bike.

A chill ran down my back. I looked at Jeff's dirty blond hair and his scraggly beard and felt as if a big invisible wall had just arisen between us. "She's fine. Perfectly fine," I heard myself say. I felt strange and alone behind the wall. I wondered if Jeff could see it.

"But what happened? How come she's in the hospital?"

"The hospital," I said, sounding bored, "it's a great place to take a rest."

"Lisl, stop kidding. What happened?" Jeff said, looking concerned.

"She had a small operation. It was, as they say on TV, strictly routine. She'll be out in a few weeks spanking new and back to business as usual."

"Sorry Lisl! I guess I was more worried than you." Jeff gave me his usual punch in the stomach and laughed with relief. The invisible wall cushioned the blow, and I hardly felt a thing.

In fact, I hardly felt anything at school all that day or for the next few days. One or two other people asked about my mom, but as soon as they heard that the operation was successful, they left me alone. Each day I sat through my classes behind the invisible wall and patiently waited for the end of school when I could visit my mom.

Just as I had expected her to, my mom was getting better every day. About a week after her operation, I helped her take her first walk. She was still connected to an IV tube that was feeding her liquid food, so I pushed it alongside as she leaned on me.

"I look like a creature from outer space," she said as we inched down the corridor together—me attached to her and she attached to the pole and the tube.

"Yeah." I laughed, but the laughter shattered

29

like broken glass against the wall and fell at my feet. I couldn't figure out why the wall wouldn't go away. My mother was getting better and cheerier. Yet, as she did, I felt further and further away from her and from everyone else.

The next day was Saturday, and I had planned on spending the whole day at the hospital with my mom. But when I woke up, I felt this strange compulsion to visit the pond, my old haunt. It was something I hadn't done since I was a kid. I packed the same gear I used to take when I was twelve—a tin can, a shovel, some string, a cork, and a safetypin—and walked the several blocks to the park.

The pond was cold and still and mostly crusted over with a combination of ice and mud. Early in the day it always smelled cold and deep. Later on, especially in the summer, it smelled damp and evil. A few grayish-brown ducks still navigated through the mud and bobbed their heads down into the water to eat or drink.

I took out my rusty metal shovel and dug for worms. Under the old twisted trees that surrounded the pond, under the pockets of ice, the earth was dark and wet. If I got lucky, I could plunge my shovel in and emerge with a clump of earth and three or four slippery worms weaving in and out of the deep brown dirt. When I was little and feeling especially brave, I picked them out individually and dropped them into the tin can. But this day I just dropped the worms and the earth in together.

30

I found a good flat rock and sat down. I drew out my string, attached it to the safety pin, and baited my hook with a wriggler. That was hard—sticking a pin through a squirming body. But I knew worms had no feelings, not like people. And worms went on living even if you accidentally sliced them in half. The two parts still wriggled about, and instead of just one worm, you suddenly had two. It was strange to realize that those rubbery, slippery tiny strands were stronger than people, stronger even than my mother. "The worms crawl in, the worms crawl out. . . ." The words to that whining song kept repeating in my head. Worms outlived human beings. They were what got you in the end. Long after you were buried in the ground, worms nibbled at your flesh and picked your skeleton clean. How horrible! I didn't know why my head was so full of such gruesome thoughts. I'd baited hundreds of hooks and never thought such things before.

I stood up, spread out my legs, and tossed the string as far as it would go—about three feet. I looked out at the pond and saw my reflection gazing back at me through the ripples. Moving back and forth in the water was a thin, small-breasted girl with long, thick black hair and bangs. I winked at her, and she winked back. In the pond, she wasn't all that bad-looking. In fact she was even a little pretty. In the middle of the face a cork was popping up and down in an even kind of rhythm. I sat down on my rock and stared at the cork and fell into a trancelike relaxation. The sun grew brighter and warmed me up. I felt cozy and comfortable and nice. Some little kids came out to poke about, but they didn't bother me.

After a couple of hours, I came to. I felt completely rested. I still hadn't caught anything, but then I hadn't really expected to. I'd never seen anyone catch anything except for an old beer can or some bottom grass. All the same, fishing at the pond was as peaceful as it had been years before. I emptied my can under the trees and watched the worms work their way back into the soil. They seemed glad to get back home.

I turned away and started back to *my* home, walking with my head squinched down in my jacket. I didn't want anyone to recognize me and ask what I'd been doing all alone at the pond. Fishing? At my age? It was all too silly to explain. Suddenly I felt nervous. My body tightened up, and before I knew what was happening, I felt enclosed again. Safe, surrounded, and a little bit lonely. It was the wall, I realized. I hadn't noticed it, but while I was "fishing," the wall had disappeared. But now it was back, and I felt nothing again.

On a Saturday exactly three weeks later, I sat in the living room with my family, waiting. My mom, who'd come home from the hospital a week before, wore a long navy-blue lounging robe trimmed in bright red. She had arranged herself as gracefully as possible on the long couch, and only once in a while did she succumb to leaning back. "Jane, is the tea all set?" she asked. She seemed determined to play the charming hostess despite the pain she still felt from the operation.

"Everything except the hot water," Jane beamed. "You look so lovely today—absolutely chic. Blue is the perfect color for you." Jane was babbling nervously, about how much better my mother looked, what a beautiful day it was, and how great it was to be all together again. She and Jim had come up for the weekend, bearing gifts. The navy-blue lounging robe had cost them a bunch, but Jane quietly confided that it had been hard to find something that would cover Mom's incision and still maintain her elegant image.

So we sat, Jane babbling, Jim nervously thumbing through one of his literary-criticism books, my father fascinated by his nails, and I on the carpet with my French book, in pain, practicing good posture and a bit of French vocabulary. My mother surveyed us all with a serenity that really unnerved me.

When the bell rang, Jane ran for it and gushed, "Well, here comes Mrs. Canby. I'm sure she'll be terrific."

Mrs. Canby was entirely Jane's idea. Jane had

phoned all over creation to find someone to come and help us "face the music" as the head social worker at the Family Service Agency so smartly put it. Mrs. Canby was arriving with highest recommendations, to help us face the music *ensemble*, as my French teacher would say. Frankly, I thought it was all a bunch of bull. Who needed some stuffy old social worker to tell us what we'd already been told—that my mom was going to die. When I heard the door open, I could just imagine the gray-haired lady with heavy shoes and a high-collared dress who would come in to lecture us on what we faced.

Instead, in strolled a girl around Jane's age, wearing a denim skirt, Mexican shirt, sandals, and a homemade shawl. Her hair was sort of softly wild, and her nose curled up to the ceiling as if it had been pinned there. Jane gazed at her in obvious shock. For once, words failed her and she didn't utter a single syllable of introduction. My father slumped in his chair, Jim glared dreadfully at Jane, and my mother tried desperately to compose herself.

"I'm Mrs. Canby," announced the girl in the shawl. "And I can see that the agency didn't warn you about my age."

"I like your shawl, Mrs. Canby," I whined, hating her for her self-confidence. "I suppose you crocheted it *all by yourself,*" I added in a taunting voice, thinking of the notorious patience and endurance of social workers.

Jane's eyes rolled about in her head as she signaled to me to shut up, but Mrs. Canby replied, "As a matter of fact, I didn't. It's my mother-in-law's creation. She's always afraid I won't look presentable," she grinned mischievously. "By the way, you can call me Sam if you like. Samantha's too long, and Mrs. Canby seems a little inappropriate." I felt vanquished and shamed, so I smiled back at her—a tiny real smile.

The first thing Sam did was ask us to introduce ourselves by our first names. Hearing her call my mom "Jean" and my dad "Louis" sounded really strange. The stuffed chair that had been reserved for "Mrs. Canby" was ignored, and somehow Sam ended up on the floor next to me.

"My specialty is dealing with families," she explained. "But I must admit I've never worked with a cancer family before. So, we'll *all* be learning together."

"Worked with," "cancer family," "learning together"? I was trying to like Samantha Canby, and it wasn't hard, but all that jargon really put me off—especially coming from someone no older than Jane. Before I knew what was happening, I stood up and in my most gracious voice said, "Mrs. Canby, I mean Sam, it's been really nice meeting you, but I think we can manage just fine on our own."

I waited for the atomic blast from my family, but amazingly, it didn't come. Instead I got the distinct feeling that we all agreed that Sam's services were not required. We would be happy to serve her some papaya mint tea, but that was where we'd like our association to end. Even Jane, judging from her unusual silence, seemed to agree.

Sam looked at each of us, and we knew she'd gotten the message. She waited a few minutes and then said, "I see. Well, I can understand how you all feel. So why don't we just try a few things today? We'll have a short talk, Mrs. Gilbert, and if it doesn't work out, we'll just forget about it. Okay?"

My mother, a little nervous, nodded her head in assent, hoping that Sam understood. Sam smiled at her. It was pretty clear that Sam understood much more than she let on.

She started with my mom. "Mrs. Gilbert— Jean—how do you feel about dying?"

My mother played nervously with her hair. "I don't feel as if I'm dying. I feel as if I'm getting better each day. Maybe I won't die," she said, with a question mark hanging heavily in the air.

"Well, what about you, Louis? How do you feel about all of this?"

My father looked up from his nails, and then his left cheek started to pucker in and out, the way it did when he was furious with me and trying to keep it in. His face turned red, and for the hundredth time he looked like he might explode. "I don't feel anything," he said finally, and stared back at his nails.

36

"I see," nodded Sam, squinting her eyes with concern. "Jim?"

With an embarrassed look on his face, Jim reached into his back pocket and pulled out a slip of yellow paper. "I'd like to read a few lines by an Indian poet I like very much. I think they will tell you how I feel, and they might even be helpful to Jean." Jim cleared his throat, glanced nervously at my mother and began. "Let me not pray to be sheltered from dangers but to be fearless in facing them./Let me not beg for the stilling of my pain but for the heart to conquer it." When he finished, he looked miserable, and Sam looked thoughtful and pleased.

As I could have predicted, Jane fell apart. This time it was a tidal wave of words that came crashing down upon us. "I can't. I won't. I won't have it. No. I don't want her to die. It's not fair. It can't be."

My mother's face became very tense, and suddenly she looked extremely tired. Jane took a deep breath and quieted down.

Sam was looking at me now. Her eyes were bright, and it felt as if she could see into me. I panicked. It was as if I were naked. But then I felt the protection of the wall around me. I looked out at Sam. She didn't frighten me now. I decided to keep her waiting. Several minutes went by. Sam didn't seem to mind waiting. Finally she said quietly, "Lisl, look at your mother. Tell her what you see."

I turned my head toward my mom. What could I say? I hated what I saw. She looked exhausted. For the first time in her life, she looked old. She had lost weight and was skinny—or maybe I was imagining it. No, she looked well. After all, there she was, sitting up in the living room in an elegant dress playing hostess. That was it. She looked fine, perfectly fine. But then I remembered the worms, and suddenly I saw only skin and bones—how she'd look when she was dead. From behind the wall I heard Sam repeat, "What do you see?" I still hadn't opened my mouth yet. I looked really hard into my mom's eyes and blocked out the rest of her body. "I see a lovely, tired face," I whispered, and broke down and sobbed.

Sam looked at me with sympathy and approval. But I had lied. I couldn't see the present anymore. The present *was* a lovely, tired face, but I saw only the future—a diseased, bony, ugly face.

"Whatever happens, and whenever it happens, you all have *now* to enjoy each other. Don't let the future ruin the present," she said, as if reading my mind. "Jean is alive and can still do things. She is still herself. Don't let yourselves miss out on *now*."

My mom started crying, and when I looked up through my tears, I saw that everyone was—even undemonstrative Dad and Sam the social worker. And all around me was a feeling of love and sharing—a feeling not all that common in our family.

A few days later, I started to have all kinds of weird feelings in my body. I felt just like my mom. I was weak, tired, and I had tiny pains in my chest right around the place where she had had her incision. I guess you could call them sympathy pains. When I lost my appetite, I decided it was time to stop playing Mademoiselle Maturity and talk to a friend. For the last few weeks I'd been telling all my friends, even Jo, that my mom was okay. She had just gone to the hospital for a minor operation. Except for my family and the doctors, I didn't know anyone who really knew what had happened. Keeping everything inside was starting to hurt.

After a lot of thought I decided to talk to Jo. Ever since junior high school Jo and I have been best friends. We've always shared everything—from clothes to secrets. We met at one of those stupid boy-meets-girl parties. We were sitting side-by-side eyeing the same boy. He smiled, walked straight toward us, and then veered sharply to the right to ask perky, pukey Patty Rappaport to dance. Jo and I looked at each other, laughed, and began to talk. We hit it off immediately.

We talked and talked. Before we knew what had happened, the party was over and it was time to go home. It had been the first time I had ever enjoyed being what my mom would call a "wallflower." But then, meeting someone like Jo doesn't happen every day, and it sure beat dancing with some dumb guy who thought he was hot stuff.

Over the years, we've gotten to the point where sometimes we don't even need words to communicate our feelings. We see something, look at each other, and know exactly what the other is thinking.

The first time I visited Jo her mother was really uptight. She's constantly cleaning, and right in front of me she started in on a lecture. "Jo, why can't you keep your room clean? It's a regular pigsty. I don't see how you can allow a friend to see it that way."

Jo saluted, answered, "Right away, Mother," and scooted out of the room into the hallway to go upstairs. I felt embarrassed in front of Jo's mom so I ran after her. But as soon as I reached the hall, I got this crazy urge. I got down on all fours and crawled up the stairs, making quiet snorting noises. A few steps above me, Jo the pig was doing exactly the same thing—making soft squealing noises. *"Oink, oink,"* she giggled. If her mother had heard us that day, I doubt she'd have ever let me visit again.

By now she and just about everyone else are

used to our antics. Our friends call us the "Bobbsey twins." My mother used to say we had excellent "rapport," but in honor of the night we met, Jo and I prefer to call it excellent "Rappaport."

I rang Jo's bell, and her mom opened the heavy blue door, dust cloth in hand, wearing her usual apron and housedress and her usual weary but benign expression. I hated her for being healthy. It didn't seem fair. "How's your mother?" she asked politely as I held my breath. It seemed as if the whole world knew about the hospital and the return home.

"Doing fine," I lied, and whisked past her up the curved, carpeted steps to Jo's bedroom before she had a chance to ask anything further.

At the top of the stairs, Jo's half-chunky/half-sexy figure lay sprawled across the carpet. Propped up on one hand, she grinned down at me like a Cheshire cat. Her mischievous face, surrounded by ringlets of curls, always reminded me of Harpo Marx.

"Hey!" she yelled.

Seeing that sunshine face, I suddenly felt all sick and strange inside. What was I going to tell her? Why had I come? "Hey," I called back weakly.

Jo's cheery smile turned upside down when she heard the way I returned our customary greeting. She jumped up, grabbed me by the arm, yanked me into her room, and slammed the door shut.

41

"What is it?" she asked, sitting me down on the bed next to her.

Face-to-face with Jo, I felt confused. I opened my mouth to speak and nothing came out.

"What *is* it?" Jo repeated, looking scared.

I took a deep breath and pushed the words out. "My mom. Cancer. Going . . . to . . . die . . . ," I said, feeling far away.

"You mean . . . ? Oh, no," Jo gasped, and burst into tears. "How long . . . ?"

"A few months, maybe," I heard myself answer as if through a long tube.

"But why didn't you tell me before?"

"I couldn't," I sighed.

Then Jo was crying in big sobs and gulps, and I ended up consoling her. I still didn't have many words to say, so we just hugged each other. Jo always thought my mom was glamorous and unique, and I think she sometimes wished we could switch mothers. Hers was the more common garden variety. Less demands and less glitter. Sometimes I, too, used to wish we could switch, but these last few weeks I'd stopped feeling that way. I wanted my mom around in any condition.

Jo lifted her head from my shoulder. Her eyes were all swollen and round and red. "You must feel terrible," she said, wiping her eyes and nose with the end of her pillow case. "And here *I* am crying. Hey . . . what's with you, Lisl? Why aren't *you* crying?" Again, I was tongue-tied. The wall was up, and I just couldn't seem to feel anything. "Hey!" Jo shouted, and took me by the shoulders. Before I knew what was happening, she was shaking me so hard it hurt.

"Stop it," I shouted.

"No!" she yelled.

"Please!" I couldn't stand it any more. She wouldn't leave me alone. She shook and shook and shook me until I finally burst into tears. "Jo . . . Jo . . . What can I do? She's going to die! She's going to die! I can't change it. I can't understand it. Why? Why? Why my mother? It doesn't make sense," I cried.

Jo held me in her arms. "I don't know. It's horrible. It's unbelievable. It's unfair." She shook her head back and forth.

"What am I going to do, Jo?"

"I don't know."

"But I won't . . . have a mother, Jo."

"I know . . . " We were both crying then. "Hey, Lisl, if it's any consolation, you've got me . . . always."

I looked up at Jo's Harpo head and felt a slow kind of warmth and quiet rising in me. The wall had fallen down, and I felt sad but relieved. Jo was right. As long as I had her for my friend, I didn't feel quite so alone. Under that slightly chunky exterior was one of the best people on the face of the earth.

"If I've got you"—I smiled as the last tear

rolled down my face—"at least there's a lot of you to have."

"Hey!" yelled Jo, looking down at her stomach, "that's not fair!" And she grabbed her pillow and slammed it over my head. I grinned at her. Suddenly I felt my first real hunger pains in weeks.

We slipped quietly downstairs to the kitchen and devoured some chocolate cake. On her way to the laundry room, Jo's mother passed through, looking full-faced and healthy. She wasn't dying and my mother was. I felt guilty for hating her, but I couldn't help it. When she saw our faces, she said nothing. I guess our faces said a lot. I don't know what she learned from them, but enough to know not to ask any more questions.

Among the rest of my friends, the truth about my mom spread faster than the most delicious gossip. Everyone seemed to decide that the best way to deal with me was to be cheerful and funny. Jokes, gags, and false gaiety greeted me wherever I went. "Lisl's seashells by the seashore," friends taunted. "Hey, Lisl, jump on my diesel and come for a ride," Jeff yelled every time he passed me on his motorbike. I knew they were all trying to be nice but the result was obnoxious. It was all a foolish and misguided attempt to spare my feelings and cheer me up. Whenever I appeared, there was an immediate hush followed by lots of mad merriment. No more laments about finals and no more worries about the future. No more talk about college, jobs, money troubles—and as for family problems? Well, they didn't exist anymore. At least, not around me.

The worst of it was that somewhere along the line the word "dead" and all words associated with it magically dropped out of the English language. My history teacher still spoke of the death of Charlemagne in the year 814. But my friends had purged all such words from their vocabularies.

A couple of weeks after I'd confessed to Jo, Jeff and I were sitting on the wall in front of the high school, swinging our feet. School was over for the week, and we were cracking up over old Mrs. Biddle and her slippery wig.

"That lady has probably just celebrated her bicentennial," I kidded. "She's a first-class bore."

"Yeah," agreed Jeff. "I wish she'd just hang it all up and croak."

Slam went his hand over his mouth and a look of misery washed over his face. "Oh, I'm sorry," he mumbled desperately. Before I could open my mouth to answer, he gurgled, "Just remembered that it's my turn to help with dinner," and he sprinted down the street fast enough to make the track team.

I was furious and hurt. This cancer business

45

was interfering with *everything*. At home, life seemed dark and unreal. And now I couldn't even have a real laugh with a real friend.

I spent the next week hidden behind my books. I got a lot of work done, but I felt pretty lonely. I finally laid down the law one day when Jeff, Abby, fat Carol, and I were eating lunch in the cafeteria, and Carol was really down. *So* down that, leaning on one hand, she shoved her peanut butter and banana sandwich in my direction with the other. I shoved it back at her and snapped like a police chief. "Okay. Out with it!"

"It's my parents," she moaned.

"Well, what about them?"

"They're tearing me apart. One minute they say I can go to music college and the next minute I can't."

"How come?"

"It's their retirement fund. If I go to college, I'll need some money from it. Every two minutes my mom says, 'Of course, you'd do *so well* with a college education.' Then two minutes later, she complains that they have to think of their future. I'm going crazy with guilt. I'll hate them and myself if I can't go to college, but I'll die of guilt if I go." Carol broke into tears and then it happened again. "Oh, I'm so sorry! I shouldn't have said anything. What a thing to complain about with what *you're* going through."

That did it. I slammed my fist down on the table and stood up on my chair. "Go to hell!" I shouted. "I've had enough of all of you—your old stupid jokes, your new vocabulary, and the "protection" you guys peddle. I don't need to be treated like a precious doll. I won't crack. What I need is my old friends—you remember them . . . honest, straight, *real*," I screamed. "I'm sick of talking to jokers who watch their language and think I can't understand or sympathize with anyone anymore just because my mother is dying. Reality won't kill me," I yelled, "but you people with your phony behavior will."

I got down off my soapbox and realized that half the cafeteria had stopped talking in order to listen to my outburst. Jeff, Abby, and fat Carol looked ashamed and I felt relieved. I wiped some tears away, pushed in my chair, and ate half of Carol's sandwich. "Carol," I said, "you're going to music college. Tell your parents to get off your back and to keep their retirement fund. Tell them to *stuff* it," I added, feeling really cocky. I knew Carol could make it on her own because I knew how badly she wanted to. You should hear her play her cello. It's enough to make you dig Haydn.

From then on, except for one or two smiling sugar babies who were too oozingly sweet for my taste anyway, everyone got the message and treated me like they had in the old days. It felt good

47

to share problems again, and wonderful to laugh. My friends were keeping me going. When I was with them, life felt like life again.

Back at home though, things were different. My mother had taken to wearing long, bright-colored scarves around her neck. When I first noticed them, I figured she was trying out some new dramatic effect. But in her long lounging clothes, the effect looked ridiculous.

One day when she was lying down on the living room couch, I gave her the old one-two: one, "You look awful in those scarves"; two, "Why don't you get rid of them?"

In the past, she would have probably given me one of her lectures on style and individuality, but this time she slowly raised herself up from the couch and gazed at me. "Do they look that bad?" she asked, her lips wavering as she spoke.

I felt terrible for being so blunt and said, "Well, no, but why do you wear them when you have such a nice long neck? It looks as if you're trying to hide something."

My mother had a peculiar look on her face. As she slowly unraveled the long scarves, it was as if she was embarrassed. Her face wore the kind of look you see in the movies when someone strips for the first time. The scarves slid slowly down her neck and fell lightly onto her lap. Her lips trembled again and she said, "Now you know why I'm wearing these ugly things."

All across her neck and down as far as I could see on her chest were tiny black crosses. I couldn't believe my eyes nor understand them, so I crept closer to see her better. The closer I came, the farther she leaned into the couch. She looked like a wounded deer. "They're radiation marks," she breathed, and one lonely tear spilled out and rolled slowly down her cheek. "They're all over my chest, too."

"What for?" I asked, feeling chills down my front. "And why *crosses?*"

"When I go for treatments, they have to know where to beam the radiation. They mark me with crosses for the exact points, but then I can't wash them away," she explained so quietly I could barely hear her.

"Oh, Mama, I'm sorry," I whispered. "I didn't know." I held both her hands and looked deep into her eyes. They had lost their liveliness and were filled with what looked like shame. "How humiliating!"

I felt selfish and stupid. While I'd been popping around with my friends trying to get them to forget about cancer and death, my mother had been quietly going for therapy. My father drove her to the hospital a few times a week where they beamed radiation through her in hopes of a "remission." That was only one of the new words I'd been learning in the last weeks. Remission was the fancy medical word for bought time. If they could create a remission, she might live a little longer. I looked at her, covered with black crosses like someone marked for some strange occult ritual, and wondered whether she thought it was worth it to have any more time. I didn't dare to ask.

We stared at one another for a long time, neither of us speaking. But somehow I knew we were saying a lot to each other. It was strange, but for the first time in my life, I could see beneath the surface. Beneath all that frenetic activity and creativity was a woman who was confused and lonely. I guess she'd always been that way, but with all the running around she did, I'd never noticed it before.

The longer I looked, the more I saw. I'd always thought of her as a superstar. She always seemed so strong. But now she looked more like a small, helpless child—as lost and unhappy as I often felt deep inside. I wished I could get back my old busy mother. I even wished she could flirt with my dates. Suddenly I wanted her to paint again, nag me to do her a favor, or even to bore me with a description of one of her meetings. But I knew it was too late—she was too tired and too weak. All I could do was try to repair the damage I had done to what little was left of her dignity.

So I yanked some invisible cord deep inside of

50

me, stood up, and took one of the colored scarves from her lap. "Let me try something," I said quietly. My mother lifted her head a bit, and I wrapped her neck in one single scarf and let one end of it dangle down gracefully across her chest. When I stood back and looked at her, I grinned. I ran for a hand mirror to show her, and a tiny smile flickered across her face.

"You're right, Lisl. That *does* look better. But are the crosses completely hidden?" she asked almost shyly.

"Completely," I said.

"Thank you," she said, and the words knocked against me like body blows.

I scooped up the rest of her scarves, helped her lie down again, and raced up to my bedroom to bury my head in my pillow. I felt frightened and at the same time empty. It was so confusing to think that underneath it all my mom was really a lonely and lost person. I didn't know what was bothering me more—seeing my mother stripped of her scarves or seeing her stripped of her superstar image.

For a long time after that, I sleepwalked through each day. It was as if I was suspended somewhere, halfway between sleeping and waking, between death and life. I guess on the outside I

51

seemed pretty much the same person, but inside something had changed. I couldn't name it, or even think about it, but I could feel it. It was like a giant lump in my chest. Sometimes the lump would make me short of breath, and I'd choke on a word. Sometimes it would feel like a huge weight bearing down on me until it was hard to walk. Other times it felt like the kind of fear you feel before a big exam or a dentist appointment. But whatever form it took, it was always with me.

At school, I slid through classes only half there. I could still joke with my friends but my mind was somewhere else, in a place that had no focus and no name. Every few minutes I had to catch myself when I realized I hadn't heard something a teacher had said. And several times I had to borrow notes from a classmate to pick up the things I'd missed.

One day when I was sitting in my accelerated English class, I felt a tap on my back. I turned to see Andrew Guth's pimply face peering at me through thick glasses, his eyes signaling wildly for me to pay attention. I didn't know what he was trying to do until Mr. Mittleman's voice boomed through the tiny classroom, "Ms. Gilbert, have you heard *any*thing I've just said?"

I looked up into Mr. Mittleman's heavy round face and saw that his normal twinkle had disappeared and he wore a look of annoyance mixed with concern.

I liked his class. It was for us "gifted" kids who were on our way to college. If we did well, we had the chance to skip freshman English. It was fun discussing ideas and reading books, and I enjoyed the frequent writing assignments. I liked to think and wonder about things. In Mittleman's class there was rarely a "correct" answer to anything. Every question had several answers. There were always several ways of looking at and thinking about one idea. The year of Charlemagne's death was the kind of thing I had trouble remembering and could live without knowing, but reading about other people was my idea of fun. It felt warm and lovely to move through someone's writing into a world I didn't know.

I think I blushed for the first time in my life. My face felt hot and tingly. There was nothing I could say except a meek "I'm sorry."

Mittleman looked at me for what seemed like an eternity. Everyone else did the same. My head started to bend forward, and I stared blankly at my desk.

"See me after class," Mr. Mittleman boomed in his most ponderous tone. I looked up and nodded, and the class continued. The lump had grown so large I could barely breathe.

By the time the bell rang, I was sure I wouldn't be able to speak. As everyone filed out, I could feel their sympathetic glances. Even Andrew Guth stuck out his clammy hand and patted me on the shoulder. None of us had ever seen Mr. Mittleman angry, and I was privileged to be the first. When the last kid had staggered out, Mittleman waddled to the door, closed it, slowly moved down the aisle, and sat down on the front of his desk.

Then he boomed, "One of my best pupils—what's happening? Am I boring you suddenly?"

My eyes filled with tears. The compliment only made things harder. I'd let him down, and he didn't deserve it. My head was filled with all kinds of things I wanted to say about how I enjoyed him, but all I could do was say, "No, you're not." That horrible lump had reached clear up into my throat.

"Are you worried about college?" he asked, looking concerned.

How could I tell him? Sure I was worried about college . . . I guessed. In the last months I hadn't really had time to think about next year. All around me everyone else was going berserk with "Will I get in?" and "How did your interview go?" but I'd slipped away from it all. The future seemed irrelevant now. I was just trying to get through each day, and now I realized I wasn't even doing that very well.

Mr. Mittleman cleared his throat. I still hadn't answered his question. I looked into the pudgy kind face and thought that maybe I would explain everything to him. But all I could manage was, "No, it isn't college."

"Well," he said, folding up his glasses, "Not

terribly communicative. You've hardly given me any information. Anything else you want to add?"

I forced the lump down into my stomach away from my throat and said, "Just that I'm truly sorry. I've been having trouble paying attention lately. But it's been in *all* of my classes," I added quickly. "I feel the worst about yours. I promise it won't happen again."

Mittleman dabbed some perspiration off his forehead. It was a warm day, but he managed to sweat even in the middle of blizzards. "All right," he said and smiled as if we'd made a pact. "Let me tell you what you slept through. It's a special assignment, and I expect you to do particularly well on it in view of the preceding." He waved his hand in his most professorial manner as if to dismiss all of the previous bad feeling. "The Voice of Freedom Contest is held every year and this year I'm requiring all of you to enter it. By May fifteenth, I want you to write an articulate, coherent essay on 'What Freedom Means To Me.' In exchange for my understanding temperament," he twinkled, "I want *your* essay to be outstanding."

Then he reached out and covered my hand with his big, round one and said gently, "Why don't you talk to someone about whatever it is that's bothering you? That might help us both."

I nodded, wondering who in the world I could talk to when a vision of Sam Canby flashed before my eyes. I stretched my mouth into what I hoped looked like a smile, mumbled my thanks, and excused myself. When I closed the door, Mr. Mittleman was still sitting awkwardly on his desk, staring after me.

Sam's office wasn't really an office at all. It was downtown in one of those nondescript contemporary brick buildings that are filled with doctors, dentists, and young girls in starched white uniforms. The agency occupied one whole floor. It was a maze of efficient-looking desks "manned" by efficient-looking women. But when I walked into Sam's office, it looked like a tiny living room. There were two chairs, a couch, a tiny old-fashioned school desk, a Mexican rug, and some Picasso prints on the wall.

I felt confused. Which was her chair? Where was I supposed to sit? "Sit anywhere you like," Sam said, reading my mind. I chose the couch. Sam chose a swivel chair. She spun around in it and magically produced a pot of coffee. "Want some?"

"No thanks," I said nervously. It was all too much for me. This was not my idea of a social worker's behavior, and it surely wasn't what I expected of her office. But then Sam certainly wasn't a normal social worker, though I was beginning to realize I had no idea of what a normal social worker was.

She poured herself a cup, heaped about four teaspoons of sugar into it, stirred it, and settled back in her chair. "I'm glad you decided to come," she smiled. "Now, what's the trouble?"

Just as I was about to speak, that same choking lumpy feeling came back into my throat. I swallowed, trying to force it away, but it only got bigger. "I don't . . . I can't . . . I . . ." Then a kind of belching sob came out of my mouth, and I started to cry. Right there in Sam the social worker's office. It was humiliating, but I couldn't stop. When I dared look up at her, I saw an expression on her face that told me I didn't have to feel embarrassed. It almost looked as if she had expected me to fall apart. When I finished, she handed me a big box of light green Kleenex and asked if I felt any better.

"A little," I said, wiping my eyes and blowing my nose into what now looked like shredded lettuce.

"Try and tell me what's bothering you," she said gently.

"Everything," I choked. "It's more than my mother dying. It's me. I feel like I'm dying, too. I can't seem to pay attention to things. I feel like nothing. I mean like I am nothing."

"Nothing?" asked Sam.

"I've always been a nothing. I've never been

57

special like my mom. I've never been anything. *She's* the talented special one. Here I am well and strong while my mother is dying. It's not fair. It should be the other way around. It should be me."

Sam sat for a moment as if she was trying to figure something out. "You don't think you're important . . . ?"

"Not special," I said.

"I see. Well, if you don't think you're all that special, what do you plan to do about it? I mean in the future—is there anything special you plan to do, or be?"

I'd never really thought much about the future. I knew what I was, but not what I wanted to be. Then I remembered college. *That* was something. "I'm going to college next year," I announced. "It's all set. I was accepted early decision with a scholarship, and I'm going. But I have no idea what I'm going to study. I'm not even smart enough to know that. I mean, how can you be smart if you don't even know what you want to study or what you want to be?"

"Maybe the first thing to know is who you are," Sam offered.

"But I know who I am. I told you. A nothing. There's nothing special about me. It's my mom who's special. She's always been. No one can top her."

"Do you have to *top* her?" Sam asked, swiveling around in her chair and staring very

58

hard at me. "Maybe you've spent so much time trying to be like her, trying to top her, that you haven't had the time to find out what's special about yourself." Her face wore a quizzical look, and she smiled at me as if she was offering a challenge.

"Okay. So what's so special about me?" I asked in a smart-aleck tone.

"That's what *you're* going to have to find out."

"Then what good does it do to talk to you if you won't give me any answers?" I asked angrily.

"I give you questions. *You* have to find the answers," Sam smiled again. "The answers are there if you're willing to look for them."

"But what if I don't find them?" I asked miserably.

"You will. Give yourself some time. Call me in a few weeks and we'll talk and see if you've found any. Okay?"

"Okay," I answered, feeling sad and confused.

Then Sam got up, put her arm around me, and led me to the door. She smiled and I left the office.

When I got home, I lay down on my bed and thought about what Sam had said. I had absolutely no idea what was special or unique about me, but I had this funny feeling that Sam already knew. The more I tried to figure out the answer to Sam's question, the more confused I became. In desperation I finally decided to call Jo and tell her about my conversation with Sam.

"I have to find out how I'm special—who I am."

"Well, *I* know who you are."

"Who?" I asked with excitement.

"An idiot."

"Hey, Jo. Don't mess around. This is serious."

"Okay. It's just that this all seems dumb to me because I know who you are—my friend."

"Thanks. But, no insult, that's not enough. I have to find out what's special about me, what I'm *good for* and *good at*."

"Well, *good luck!*" teased Jo.

"You're as much help as Mrs. Canby was."

"What are friends for?"

It was no use. The conversation degenerated into laughter. I hung up. I was just as confused as before but a whole lot happier.

At home, things were anything but happy. My mom seemed to have lost interest in just about everything. My dad had been laid off again. He's an administrator for the City Housing Administration, and it seems like every few years they "reevaluate" the budget and lay him and a bunch of other people off. Every time it happened, my mom would get upset. She would get teary and

60

nervous and worry about how the bills would get paid. But this time she hardly seemed to notice.

About a week after I saw Sam, I came home from school and found my father studying the employment page of the newspaper while my mom lay on the living-room couch. She wasn't exactly asleep, but she wasn't exactly awake either. Dr. Traynor was giving her painkillers now, and they kept her constantly drowsy.

"How are you doing?" I asked no one in particular.

"Fine. Fine," my father's voice responded from behind the newspaper.

"He hardly ever talks. I guess he doesn't love me," my mother called weakly from the couch. My father just grumbled behind his paper.

"Of course he does," I said. Damn it. I couldn't deal with that business today. "Got to study now," I said. I started up the stairs to my room, but then I stopped halfway and looked again at the strange tableau. My father sat opposite my mom hidden behind the newspaper, not really reading it. My mother lay there, not really seeing anything. Neither spoke, and a thick silence filled the room like a huge barrier between them.

I wondered how they had fallen in love. They were complete opposites. My mom was aggressive and demanding. My dad was silent and locked up. It seemed that they were destined to make each other unhappy. I wished my father was more demonstrative. I wished my mother was more patient. If only she would try to unlock the door that was so tightly closed around him. I knew she never would. For some crazy reason, she was forever convinced that he didn't love her. In fact, that none of us did. I'd always known how Jane and I felt, and though I'd sometimes wondered about my father, I knew that deep down he loved her too.

Standing on the steps and seeing my mother motionless for so long made me feel uncomfortable. Seeing her motionless in front of my father made my skin all cold and prickly. Suddenly I realized that I'd never seen the two of them alone together without my mom scurrying about preparing to go to her next activity. There they were, sitting quietly together, yet the room screamed with their separateness.

I remembered the day with the scarves—how I'd realized that behind all that activity was a lonely lost person. I thought about what Sam and I had talked about. Suddenly it hit me that my mom and I were alike. We *both* didn't know who we were. If my mom knew who she was, she'd know how much we loved her. She wouldn't have had to run around so much. Maybe she would never have gotten sick. My head felt dizzy with all these new strange thoughts.

I looked out past my parents into the living room. On the wall above the couch was one of my mom's paintings. It was a magnificent blue, green, and gray thing that showed sailboats tossed about in a storm. Two years before, it had won second prize in an art show. I loved it, and so had the judges on the art committee. But my mom had never been pleased. In fact, she said the judges had given her the prize because hers was the only "semirealistic" painting in the show.

And a year ago, when she finally got the job she'd always wanted—teaching art history at the local college—she called it "tokenism." My dad took us out to dinner to celebrate, but the evening ended with my mother angrily staring at my silent father and debating with Jane and me: "The only reason they selected me was because they needed a female teacher among all those men." True or not, it never occurred to her that they'd selected her from twenty applicants—male *and* female, and they'd done it because they thought she was the best.

Suddenly I realized that, inside, Mom the superstar felt as much like a nothing as I did. It seemed incredible and impossible—she was so talented. Then a disturbing, unnerving thought crossed my mind. Maybe I, too, was talented. Maybe even creative. Maybe I just didn't know it. Sam was probably right. Maybe I'd been too busy trying to be like my mom to know what or who *I* was. I knew one thing for sure, though. For the first time in my life, I didn't want to be like my mom—

running as fast as I could to get away from myself, never stopping long enough to know what was good or unique about me. I wanted some peace in my life and I figured the only way to get it was to find out who I was and what was special about me. Those were Sam's questions, I realized, and I still hadn't found the answers, but at least I had started thinking about them. I walked slowly up the rest of the stairs. I didn't know why, but suddenly I felt very tired and a little old.

A few days later, I sat in my room surrounded by torn-up paper, scribbled notes, and broken pencils. I was completely stuck. May fifteenth was fast approaching, and I had done nothing about the Voice of Freedom Contest. It was the first time I'd ever had trouble when it came to writing anything. But each time I sat down to start "What Freedom Means to Me" I heard Mr. Mittleman's heavy tones exhorting me to write something brilliant. As soon as I heard that voice, I felt paralyzed. Who knew what freedom was? And what in the world did it mean to me? It was all too abstract. Besides, I knew what the Voice of Freedom committee wanted, and it was something I couldn't deliver.

They were an old organization filled with veterans of world wars and people who felt about the flag the same way some people feel about family heirlooms. It was as if Vietnam, Watergate, and all the other crazy things that happened in "the land of the free, and the home of the brave" had never occurred. They wanted something patriotic for their contest, and the only thing that had entered my idiot brain was "amber waves of grain." I liked that. Somehow that was the closest I could come to thinking about what freedom meant to me.

I finally decided to get out of the house and work at Jo's. I grabbed a notebook, jumped on my bike, and pedaled away. Jo went to private school, so we could never work together on assignments, but we often did our own homework together. We share the same rhythms. We get tired at the same time, goof off at the same time and sometimes work our heads off for hours without saying a single word to each other.

Fifteen minutes later I sat, pen in hand, at Jo's dainty pink desk in her dainty pink chair. (Her mother had planned her room, and I think she was thinking of Tinkerbell when she designed the place. Jo had outgrown it the day the furniture was moved in.) She lay sprawled on her bed, working on some advanced math problems, looking a bit like a small hippo luxuriating in mud.

Despite her mother's constant nagging, Jo never made her bed, so her chunky body lay almost hidden amidst bulging sheets, notebooks, and papers. In the middle of it all, an occasional stuffed animal poked its head up and inspected the general mess.

I chewed away at my nails, drowning in fear and thought. I just couldn't please those committee members and Mr. Mittleman at the same time. Finally I decided it was hopeless. I'd have to please myself and hope that it all worked out. I was still fixed on those dumb amber waves of grain but slowly I realized why. Freedom was really something quite simple—it was doing what I wanted, when I wanted to do it. Like writing my essay in my own special way. Like going where I wanted to go—straight up the ladder of success like a corporate executive or slowly wandering through fields of amber grain. I stopped chewing my nails and began:

What Freedom Means to Me

To walk through fields on a summer day. To explore faces on a crowded bus. To sleep without fear. . . . To make a new friend. To go to church or temple—or not to. To walk, arm linked with a loved one in the twilight. To smile and laugh and cry and shout. These and more are what I call freedom.

The freedom I know and treasure is living in a country whose people are as varied as pebbles on a beach. Rough and smooth; bright or dull; black, brown, red, yellow, or white; large or small; all contributing to the beauty of the whole. To be alive in such an environment is truly a gift.

Freedom of opportunity allows me to fulfill myself. I can be a teacher or a tailor, a merchant or a maid, a doctor or a ditch digger. I am my own master.

I can shout about how much I hate the world or about how much I love it. I can even tell you why. I can believe in God or gods, anything or nothing. I can believe in myself. My ideas and thoughts and deeds are as important as anyone else's.

The elements of freedom are intangible. Freedom is an emotion, deep within me, impossible to describe. Freedom is the ability to believe in myself and to live life as I choose. Freedom is *me* doing what I want to do.

When I had finished, I exhaled. I'd written straight through without stopping or changing a single word. It had just spilled out. It certainly wasn't your standard patriotic essay, but it was as close as I could get to a personal definition of freedom.

My exhale had been much louder than I thought and it pulled Jo up out of her mud bath. "Okay, let's hear it," she commanded. I cleared my throat and read it to her, awaiting her verdict.

"Interesting," she said slyly.

"What in the world does *that* mean?" I asked, annoyed by her brevity.

67

"Didn't you tell me that that Mrs. Canby asked you to find out who you are?"

"So?"

"Reread your essay, kiddo. Sounds like you're finding out."

I stared stupidly at the paper in front of me. When I reread it, I realized that I'd partially solved two problems. Good old perceptive Jo. I'd written a halfway decent essay on freedom, and right there, staring up at me in green ink, it said. "Freedom is *me* doing what I want to do." If I found out what I wanted to do, I'd be free and me! I still had no idea what I wanted to do, but this time I felt like a detective who was on the right track.

"Hey, Jo, thanks!" I yelled, grabbing my pen and my notebook.

"Hey, where do you think you're going?"

"Home."

"Some friend! The minute the pinch is over, she leaves. What about my math problems? I haven't finished *them* yet."

"You will," I yelled, skipping down the steps two at a time and out the back door. I jumped on my bike and heard a loud catcall from an upstairs window. When I looked over my shoulder, there was Jo's curly head leaning out.

"Just you wait 'Enry 'Iggins!" she shrieked.

I blew her a kiss and sailed gracefully down her driveway into the street. I pedaled real hard to the top and then coasted down the next street, letting the breeze whip my hair back against itself and inhaling the sweet smell of the spring flowers that lined the gardens of the elegant houses I passed.

I felt light-headed and free—like the captain of a ship. The bike was my vessel, and I could race it or let it drift along slowly until it almost stopped. It was silly to go home so soon. The sun was still fairly bright. I had finished my essay. There was still an hour or so before I had to make dinner. I steered my ship toward the park. Before I knew it, I was coasting down the road toward the pond.

Near the small flat rock where I had fished several months before, I pulled over, set my bike down next to me, and sat down. The ice was gone, and the pond was cool and still. Some purple and white crocuses poked their heads out of the moist ground under the trees. A few young kids were fishing for old shoes and imaginary fish in the mucky water. I couldn't believe that only a short time earlier I'd been one of them. I felt very different now. I guessed I had grown up, though I couldn't figure out when or how it had happened. I took out my notebook and reread my essay. It seemed really good. And the best part was that I'd enjoyed writing it. When I thought about it, I realized that I'd always liked writing. I liked playing around with words and thoughts. I closed my notebook and stretched out on the rock for a few minutes. Perhaps one day I'd be a famous writer. Everyone would read my books. That made me smile. The pond was a magical place. But now it was time to go home.

When I pushed open the back door to our house, I was whistling and humming and singing to myself like a crazy lady. My dad sat at the kitchen table, carefully cutting the ends off string beans. My mom no longer ate meals with us. She rarely had an appetite, so we cooked her bits of her favorite foods whenever she was hungry and able to eat.

"*You* seem happy. What's up?" my father asked, looking up from his KP.

"Oh, nothing. It's just that I wrote the Great American Essay—that's all," I bragged. My father looked puzzled. "Only kidding. It's really that I had to write something for this contest—the Voice of Freedom—and I wrote it, and I think it's probably okay."

"Good," he said, wasting no words.

"How's Mom?"

"All right, I guess," my father answered, but suddenly his face looked old. "I think she's sleeping."

I stuck my head into the living room. My mom was half-sitting, half-lying in our ugly brown reclining chair. She was flipping the pages of a magazine, but I could tell that her mind was somewhere else. She looked sad and very lonely.

"Would you like some company?" I asked.

"Oh . . . yes," she said, looking grateful.

"How's it going?"

"Not so bad today," she said in a weak voice. "Except that now I know how an athlete feels when she's been benched."

I smiled but didn't say anything. I didn't know what to say.

"What's that?" she asked, looking at my notebook.

"Oh, it's nothing—just an essay I wrote for a contest." I looked at my mother. I rarely showed her any of my work. I had learned long ago that it just wasn't worth it. She was always too busy. But now that she wasn't rushing around anymore . . . well, maybe she'd like to see it. "You can read it . . . if you want," I said shyly.

"I'd really like to, Lisl, but I'm awfully tired. I can't even read the articles in this maga—"

"Oh, don't worry about it," I said quickly. "Like I said, it's nothing—just a dumb essay. You wouldn't want to read it anyway."

"I'm too tired to read it, Lisl, but *you* could read it to me. I'd like to hear it. I really would."

"Oh . . . well . . . thanks," I said, feeling confused. "But anyway, it's getting late, and I have to make dinner."

"I'll take care of dinner tonight, Lisl," my

71

father said. He was standing quietly at the entrance to the living room. "Go ahead. It's your night off."

"Thanks," I said quietly. Life was certainly a festival of surprises.

I pulled a stool over next to my mother, cleared my throat, and started to read. My mother leaned back into her chair and closed her eyes. She looked relaxed and peaceful for the first time in ages.

"To smile and laugh and cry and shout," I read.

"What's the name of the contest?" my mother interrupted.

"The Voice of Freedom," I answered. She didn't say anything so I continued to read. When I got to the end, I looked up. My mother was half asleep.

"Lisl," she mumbled. "You're going to win." Then she reached out and patted me on the arm and fell asleep. There was a tiny, almost imperceptible smile on her lips.

"My turn," my dad said when we had finished eating dinner. He reached for my notebook. Then he peered down at my essay through his thick brown reading glasses.

"Not bad," he said when he finished.

I guess that meant "pretty good" in his abbreviated language so I felt very pleased. My mom and dad both liked my essay. It was time for a celebration. I deserved a reward.

72

It seemed like ages since I'd been out on a date, and I decided that Bobby Gomez was the reward I wanted. He's tall, dark, and beautiful, and though I smile at him whenever I can, he never seems to notice me. I figure it can all be explained by the theory about opposites attracting. I'm dark and he's dark, and whenever I see him, he's with some blonde-haired beauty like Patty Rappaport. He's class president and one of the most popular guys in school. From time to time he says hello to me, and whenever he does, I get all flustered and scared. By the time I pull myself together he's usually halfway down the hall. It's obvious that I'm not the object of his romantic fantasies. On the other hand, he's definitely the object of mine. I just knew he'd like me if only he had the chance to get to know my sparkling personality. After all, looks aren't everything. Not everyone can be Miss America. Some of us have to be content to be Miss Congeniality—or a runner-up.

So I summoned up all my courage and decided to call him and ask him out. After all, if I didn't call him first, by the time Bobby Gomez realized we were meant for each other, we might both be old and gray.

I sat down, took a deep breath, reached for the phone, and started to dial. It wasn't until I heard the first ring that I realized I'd made an incredible mistake. I had dialed the wrong number and had called good old Bruce Bomes instead of Bobby

Gomez. I knew it was either "a Freudian slip" or a case of chickening out, but before I could hang up, there was that familiar bland voice at the other end of the phone.

"Yeah?" he whined.

"What a way to answer the phone!" I moaned. "Don't you even know how to say hello?"

"Who *is* this? Oh, never mind. I recognize the silver tones and the sweet temperament. How are you? And what do you want after all this time?"

I felt a little ashamed. After all, it wasn't his fault that I'd called him instead of Bobby Gomez. "I'm sorry," I said. "I guess I'm in a bad mood."

"Yeah. It's okay. I heard about your mom. That's pretty depressing. She's an unusual lady, and I'm—"

"Would you like to go out?" I interrupted, desperately trying to change the subject. "I mean to a movie or something?"

"Sure. There's a great disaster film I'd like to see. I'll even be a sport and treat you."

Leave it to Bruce Bomes to love disaster movies. I hate them. When we used to date, we could never agree on anything. I'd want to see a basketball game, and he'd want to go bowling. But this time, I figured, he was paying, so I said okay.

The movie was a disaster in every sense of the word. The earth quaked, buildings collapsed and burst into flames, planes crashed, and well-dressed women with not a hair out of place raced in terror

74

from looting rampaging men. It was ridiculous and a thousand times worse than I could have imagined. When it was finally over, the curtain closed on Houston, Texas, as a vast wasteland. I walked up the aisle next to Bruce Bomes in total silence.

My eyes slowly adjusted to the bright lights in the lobby, and Bruce Bomes put his arm around me, steered me through the crowds, and whispered, "Sorry." I couldn't answer him. I couldn't even be civil, I was in such a lousy mood. It wasn't just the stupid movie. It was him. Every time I looked at him, I remembered how he used to visit my mom and sip papaya mint tea with her, back in what I now thought of as the good old days. I felt jealous and sad at the same time. Jealous that he had found my mom so interesting and sad that he'd never be able to visit her like that again. My mind wandered all over the place, and I hardly heard anything he said.

We were drinking thick shakes in Friendly's when Bruce Bomes slammed his fist down on the counter and yelled, "Lisl, what's the matter with you? You haven't listened to anything I've said all night. I know you're not exactly in love with me, but you could at least pay attention. After all, *you* asked *me* out."

"I'm sorry," I said, feeling terrible and apologizing for the second time. "I just can't seem to concentrate. I should never have called you."

"It's your mom, isn't it?"

"Yes," I confessed, embarrassed that I was being so transparent. "I keep remembering how you used to come over to visit her after we stopped dating."

"Yeah. Well, how else was I supposed to see you?"

"I . . . You mean you came to see *me* and not my mom?"

"Well, of course. I had to try *some*thing. I mean, your mom's terrific and all, but she's a little on the old side for me. I figured if I hung around long enough and pretended I didn't care about you, you might get interested in me again. You know— reverse psychology? Only it didn't work . . . or did it? Hey . . . how come you called tonight?"

"Oh, I don't know. I guess I missed you a little," I lied, feeling confused and figuring maybe I should start being polite.

"Well, it's about time! I hope you aren't mad about the movie."

"No," I lied again.

"Well, I'm sorry if I yelled at you. But I didn't realize how upset you were about your mom. Don't feel bad. You're a pretty tough nut. If it was me, I'd be off the wall by now. Did you at least enjoy the shake?" he asked as we started home.

"Yes," I said, "and thanks."

Bruce Bomes was actually pretty considerate and understanding. It was strange that I'd never

76

noticed before. I felt weird and confused. All those visits with my mom had really been on account of me? How come I hadn't realized? Maybe tonight wasn't the only time I hadn't paid attention to him. Maybe I had *never* really paid attention to him.

In the days when we used to go out I spent most of my time comparing him with other people—wishing he was someone else—someone handsome like Bobby Gomez. We always had a good time together because I always felt comfortable with him—as if he was an old friend. But I'd never really focused on him. I'd never slowed down long enough to see him. Sure I'd seen his big ears and his short funny nose, but I'd never tried to see *inside* him. When I let myself think about it, I realized that he was more than a nice guy. He was considerate and sensitive, and most important, he seemed to care about me. And, really, he wasn't all that bad-looking. He had a pleasant face and a warm smile. When we said good night, I kissed him on the cheek and thanked him for putting up with me. He looked very uncomfortable. I think he knew that, for the first time ever in our relationship, I wasn't being a smart-aleck. I meant what I said.

A few days later, I was hurrying down the corridor on my way to French when Jeff stopped me, all excited. "Got a great rumor to share."

"Not now. I'll be late for French class."

"It's about *you*, dumbo."

"What is it?" I asked, feeling heat spreading across my forehead. All I could think of was that Bruce Bomes had told him about our date.

"Now you can really start blushing. Your essay was chosen to represent the high school in the Voice of Freedom Contest! The word is they thought it was unique and poetic. Mittleman's in heaven that it was one of his students." Jeff grinned all over, punched me lightly in the stomach, and taunted, "Don't be late for French."

I hardly had time for the shock I felt. Five minutes after I sat down in French class and opened up my *Petit Vocabulaire*, a messenger came in requesting Madame Ellis to release me from class so that I could meet with Mrs. King, the dramatics coach.

Mrs. King was a tiny, middle-aged black woman with long gray hair that cascaded down her shoulders and back. She always came to school loaded down with silver. It hung from her ears, her neck, her wrists, and crawled up the sleeves of her tentlike dresses. Her voice was high and bell-like, and she spoke as she dressed—like a young, clever actress. She whipped up a senior play as fast as a magic chef. We called her "the black tornado."

It was apparently her job to teach me how to enunciate, project, and read my golden essay with feeling, so that I could win the contest for the

78

school. The competition was just two days away at a downtown radio station where they planned to tape each "representative" reading his or her essay. The winner would be on the radio!

I was scared to death. This was too much. For two days Mrs. King drilled me in how to say simple words like "to" without an accent. (I didn't know I had one.) I was to "lift my voice" on the word "shout" when I read the line, "To smile and laugh and cry and shout." In fact, I had to act out *all* those dumb words. I found myself grimacing like a loon, smiling like an idiot, and puckering my face when I came to the word "cry."

Mrs. King patiently urged me to be more subtle. "Raise your eyes from the paper and gaze out at the judges," she urged. "Imagine that you are speaking to each one of them in-di-vid-u-al-ly," she enunciated. Every time I looked up and tried to imagine them, I choked on a word. If writing this noble essay had been easy, delivering it was another matter. Suddenly my words seemed meaningless and it was all I could do to keep from laughing. But Mrs. King pressed on, wildly waving her arms like a mad conductor. "Mod-u-late," she commanded. So I tried to lower my normally shrill voice. Finally I was able to read the whole mess out loud with the same emotions I'd felt when I'd written it.

"Bravo!" she cried. "A beau-ti-ful speech, brilliantly spoken."

I took a deep bow. Mrs. King curtsied. She had definitely missed her calling. She belonged on Broadway.

On the day of the contest, she sat perfectly erect in the studio audience, her silver jewelry lighting her dark face. Next to her sat Mr. Mittleman and Mr. Donahue, the vice-principal. Mittleman, as usual, was mopping his brow. I couldn't tell if it was the heat or nervousness. Mr. Donahue, with his skinny green bow tie and red skin, beamed with pride as if *he'd* written my essay.

The first contestant was a perfect-looking girl—perfect hair, perfect skin, perfect clothes. She mounted the steps to the podium in graceful, assured strides, beamed sweetly at the audience, quietly cleared her throat and began, "America is the land of the free, the home of the brave."

I thought I'd throw up. I could imagine Mr. Mittleman yelling, "trite, hackneyed, unoriginal." But Miss Perfection spoke beautifully, not once glancing down at her paper. Instead, she took turns gazing at everyone in the audience and smiling as she spoke. By the time she finished, I was sure she had thoroughly charmed the judges, who sat stiffly in the front row trying very hard to look important and attentive.

A few other people followed. Their speeches seemed to blend together into one long soothing drone. Before I knew it, my eyes closed and my mind drifted far away to a pine forest where crickets and birds beat out a crazy rhythm and chirped and sang in strange harmony. I sat, feeling pleasantly drowsy, in front of a big warm campfire that hissed and crackled so noisily it made me open my eyes, just in time to discover that the crackling fire was really applause, and the hissing was Mr. Donahue trying desperately to get my attention. My name and school had just been announced. Miraculously my legs lifted me up out of my seat, carried me toward the steps and up, with an almost unnoticeable stumble, to the podium.

I gazed out at what now looked like a huge theater full of people and located Mrs. King who smiled reassuringly at me. I remembered her instructions—pause, speak slowly, mod-u-late. "To walk through fields (excitement) on a summer day. To explore (curiosity) faces on a crowded bus. To sleep (pause, with earnestness) without fear. . . ." I began, and before I knew it, I was saying with real conviction, "Freedom is *me* doing what I want to do." There was a burst of applause that I was sure sounded louder than the polite clapping that had followed the previous contestants. The judges, however, continued to look sober and noncommittal.

The last contestant was a skinny broomstick of a boy obviously wearing his Sunday suit. No one had had to tell *him* to stand straight. He moved as

81

if he was wired for perfect posture. His Adams apple moved up toward his chin as he raised his hand and pointed his finger at the rest of us. "Give me liberty . . . or give me death," he began, and then paused for what seemed like five minutes as this profound new thought was given time to sink into all our heavy heads.

The rest of his speech contained every *cliché* I'd ever heard Mittleman object to. And the grand finale was, you guessed it, "And so I remind you of those immortal words, 'Give me liberty or . . . give me *death!*' "

The word "death" reverberated through the studio like a challenge. I think the guy was sincerely begging God or someone to let him keel over right then and there on the podium. Anything to emphasize his point. I couldn't believe his nerve or stupidity. He had copped his speech from every historical figure in American history. I wished I had a huge cream pie to hit him in the face with the next time he asked for it. But I retained my decorum and politely applauded.

After stale cookies, bland punch, and congratulations from Mr. Mittleman, Mrs. King, and even stuffy Mr. Donahue (all of whom were convinced "we'd" win), I returned to my seat to hear the verdict.

It was for Patrick Henry, whose Adam's apple rose at exactly the same moment that he did, to accept the coveted Voice of Freedom plaque and the opportunity to blitz our community with his boring trite speech via the miracle of radio. The judges looked extremely pleased with themselves. I think they felt assured that they'd preserved democracy and freedom for yet another year.

As Madame Ellis would say at the end of class, "*C'est tout.*" I left with King, Mittleman, and Donahue mumbling about poor taste and un-originality. As for me, I was relieved that it was over. I'd known those judges wouldn't appreciate me, and besides, I couldn't imagine that any of them had *ever* walked through fields, even on a spring day. I felt strangely clean and satisfied— sort of pure. I didn't need a plaque. I knew my speech had been good, and I felt light-headed at the realization.

The kids at school were wonderful about the contest. They nicknamed me "the writer" and teased me incessantly. But behind it all, I felt their admiration, and it felt warm and wonderful. It was really nice to be admired for something other than my big mouth or my sense of humor.

Somehow Jane and Jim had also found out about my speech. It must have been my dad who told them. The first person I told was my mom, but it had been on one of her bad days so she didn't seem to hear me. When I told my dad, he just nodded and smiled. It seemed to me that he didn't care all that much, but I guess silent dad had been a little excited and pleased with me after all. Jane and Jim called long distance and were full of words like "proud," "excited," "happy," etc. It was embarrassing, but it sure was nice.

I decided to see Sam again. I wanted to tell her my news. Though I hadn't seen her for quite some time, I had this strange sensation that she had been with me all along. Sort of the way a friend is with you even when they're really not. I guess, beneath it all, I liked her. Also, I had this sneaky feeling that I'd finally found some answers to her questions. I couldn't figure out what they were exactly, but I thought I had some idea, and so I decided to talk to her again.

Sam's eyes penetrated my face like a searchlight as she opened the door to her office. Then her lips curled up at the corners into a mischievous smile that matched her upturned nose and the ringlets of her hair. "You look awfully pleased with yourself," she said, her voice lifting at the end of the sentence to form a slight question.

"Yes," I said, "I guess I am." And I sat down in the swivel chair Sam had used during my first appointment. She watched carefully and then sat down opposite me on the couch cross-legged, looking pleased and contented.

"Well, what's up?"

Suddenly I felt shy and embarrassed. I mean,

who cared about a dumb old Voice of Freedom
Contest? Besides, Sam was someone you told
*un*happy things to. There were still plenty of those
around, so I told her about my mom, that she was
sicker and thinner every day, how each day she
seemed further and further away from us. That my
father had lost his job and couldn't seem to reach
out to her. How lonely she seemed. How lonely he
seemed. How soon she would probably die. How
my dad would be left all alone. How I thought that
deep inside, my mother might have always felt like
me—like a big nothing.

"But what about *you*?" Sam interrupted. "You
haven't told me anything about you?"

"Nothing much to say," I said, swiveling back
and forth in the chair. "I try to help, but it's harder
and harder." I looked up at Sam whose eyes were
like an X-ray machine. I could tell from the look on
her face that she knew I was holding something
back. "I won, I mean I lost the Voice of Freedom
Contest," I said, feeling shy.

"You won it, but you lost it?" Sam asked,
laughing. "I think you'd better explain that one.
For some reason, I don't follow you."

Sam's laugh made me relax. I told her about
the essay and the contest. Why it didn't matter to
me that I'd lost. Why, in a funny kind of a way, I
felt as if I'd won.

The next thing I knew, Sam asked me if I
minded reciting the speech to her. I had it almost

85

memorized by then, so she got the full performance, a few lines out of order, with all of Mrs. King's facial gestures included. When I had finished, Sam was deep into one of her silences again. I was starting to feel uncomfortable when she spoke.

"*That* was *really* wonderful," she said slowly. "Seems to me you've learned something."

I wrinkled my nose in disgust. Back to business. *Learned* something? It was only a dumb, old speech. This social-work stuff was starting to get on my nerves again. But then I remembered Jo's voice saying, "Sounds like you're finding out who you are." And the last line of the essay floated back to me: "Freedom is *me* doing what I want to do."

"The kids in school have been calling me 'the writer,' " I began. "I don't know . . . I guess I've always loved writing. Reading, too. . . ." I paused and looked at Sam. She nodded as if to ask me to continue. "This is going to sound corny, but . . . well . . . it's great to be alive. More and more every day, I've been realizing what that means. It's not so hard. I see my mom slowly closing her eyes to life, and I know that it's only a matter of time. One day there's an end to life for all of us, so we'd better enjoy it now while we can. I guess that's why I wrote about walking through fields and enjoying people. 'Cause I like those things, and they aren't forever. The biggest thing I've realized is that you don't have to do a million things to be happy—maybe just one or two. But they have to be things you enjoy. For me, that's writing. Reading. Being with friends. Maybe some things I haven't discovered yet. I guess that's how I came up with the last line of the essay."

"Then you know what you want to do now?"

"No," I said, feeling miserable again. "I'm not sure yet. I just know some things I like to do."

"The last time you were here, you said you were a nothing. Do you still feel that way?"

"No," I heard myself say.

"Well, who are you?"

My mind began fuzzing over like a cotton-candy machine, and suddenly I couldn't think any more. I hated this third-degree business.

"Who *are* you?" Sam Canby repeated.

"I'm *me!*" I shouted in anger, and we both jumped.

"You certainly are," grinned Sam, wearing the same look that Mrs. King had worn when she yelled, "Bravo!" "The last time you were here, you said there was nothing special or creative about you. It sounds as if you've changed your mind."

Now I was really confused. I hadn't even thought about being creative or special. All I knew was that recently I hadn't been feeling like a nothing. I thought and thought. Memories flashed on and off like a flickering old-time movie. The events and realizations of the last weeks replayed themselves in my mind. Standing up to people—even my good friends—and telling them off when they needed it. Discovering that my mom was no superstar. That behind that facade of glamour and confidence she really felt like a big nothing. Mittleman's challenge to write a good essay. Writing one. My friendship with Jo. Realizing how much Bruce Bomes like me. Finding out that I loved writing and was good at it. Watching my mom die—and deciding that *I* wanted to live.

I looked at Sam's crossed legs. "What's special about me is me. But that doesn't make any sense, does it?"

"Well, does it?" Sam asked, forever answering a question with a question.

"Yes," I said, suddenly feeling sure of myself. In my own way, I was special. No superstar. Just me. It felt good.

Without asking, I knew that it was time to leave. Sam kissed me as I opened the door. "Call me whenever you want to talk and don't forget what you've found out. You're special. To me, too, you know."

Talk about feeling high! I was soaring through the clouds as I left for home. Sam Canby was really something—and who could tell? Maybe so was I.

Jim and Jane came up to spend yet another

weekend with us. If I couldn't measure my mother's deterioration with my own eyes, the escalation in visits from my sister and brother-in-law would have done it for me. They knew the end was growing nearer, and I guess they wanted to get in as much time as they could before it finally came.

Part of me understood their feeling, but part of me wished I could close my eyes and erase the sight that was constantly there. The skinny-boned woman with the doll-like face bore little resemblance to the glamorous mom I'd known. It was becoming harder and harder to recall the once-elegant lady who used to greet my dates. If I could have lived away from home the way Jane did, I wondered if I would have avoided visiting my mom. That way I could have remembered her as she used to be. Every time Jane entered the door, I could see the shock she tried so hard to hide when she first glimpsed my mom. Being away even for a few weeks, she could see the change even more dramatically than I could.

It was late in May, and my mom could hardly walk. My dad, who has a bad back, and I, who am not famous for my strength, formed a human chair by weaving and lacing our hands and arms together. Each morning and every evening we'd carry my mom down and up the stairs like a frail princess. At first we joked about it, but it was all past joking now. My mother saw no humor in her total dependence on us, and we felt only fear at her weakness. She spent each day on the couch with occasional trips to the bathroom. Every trip seemed like a hike that became harder and longer. To get there and back, she had to hold herself up and lean on my dad and me. She could barely do it.

It was during one of those hikes that Jim and Jane arrived. As my dad and I slowly returned my mom to the couch, Jane backed into the kitchen out of sight. When I looked in on her, her face was white from straining with the enormous effort not to cry out. She looked at me helplessly. (My big, worldly wordy sister!) What could I do? There was nothing to say. I sat down next to her, kissed her, and held her hand.

"Thanks," Jane whispered.

It was the first time I'd ever tried, or been able, to help her—she always played Older-Sister-Who-Copes-With-All even though she wasn't all that good at it. But I guess this was too much for any of us. Jim looked exhausted all the time now. My father seemed to have aged ten years, and I was losing more and more weight so that sometimes I felt as if I'd soon be mistaken for my mom.

Jane and I were still sitting quietly together in the kitchen when suddenly we heard a faint-voiced call that made me shiver with fear. With the little breath that she had left, my mom was summoning us. Jane and I looked at each other and then jumped up and ran into the living room. My mother had succeeded in raising herself up a bit on the couch. She looked really peculiar, sort of electrified.

"I can get well," she announced in the strange whispery sound that was now her voice. "I can get well if you all help me."

Even my father registered a few degrees of shock on the Richter scale. He looked at Jim who looked at Jane and me. Help? What more could we do? We were constantly checking her, feeding her, discussing her, and watching the clock to see if it was time for her various medicines and pain-killers. I wished we were rich enough for a nurse, I could barely stand it any more.

"How can we help you?" I asked.

"Stay with me—all of you—until I get well. Don't go away." The look on my mother's face terrified me.

"But you know I have to work," Jane said weakly. "And Jim, too. We'd lose our jobs."

"Stay with me. I can't make it without you." She looked at me, and I swear her eyes were begging. "Stay home from school until I'm well. I just need some time. You can wait. Then I know I can get well," she said breathlessly.

My forehead began to tighten, and a heavy pain began pounding ferociously in rhythm with my heartbeat. Stay home from school? Then I wouldn't graduate on time. I'd have to postpone college—trade my life for hers. Maybe if I believed that kind of magic could work. . . . But *now*? I

91

just couldn't do it. For the first time ever, I valued my own life and the things I wanted to do.

I opened my mouth to say no, but my tongue stuck to the roof. My mouth was totally dry. I swallowed several times trying to generate some saliva, but all I swallowed was air. My body felt like a violin that was tuned too tightly. The strings were about to pop. Jim was standing next to me shifting heavily from one foot to the other. I could feel the floorboards moving back and forth under my feet. My father said nothing. He ran his fingers back over his hair again and again as if he was combing it. I tried to speak again.

"Mama," I said hoarsely. "I can't give up school. It's too much to ask. And Jim and Jane— they can't give up their jobs. You wouldn't want that, would you?" I asked, pleading with her to understand and forgive me.

For a long time, my mother looked at me without saying anything. My body trembled with fear. I wished she would speak. Then her head fell back on the pillow, and her eyes closed. She had fallen asleep.

I looked at Jane and Jim and my father. They looked exhausted and upset. I felt like a murderer. I was wracked with guilt, and at the same time, sorrow. That strange look! As if she actually believed she could beat death if only we would give up or postpone our lives.

Jim, Jane, and my dad went out for a walk. I

sat quietly at the edge of the couch, watching my half-dead mother sleeping. Why did she have to ask for something so impossible? I had only just begun to appreciate myself and my life. Why did standing up for myself have to be so painful? Why did it have to mean denying my mother a final wish?

"Mama," I called softly, touching her cheek and pushing her hair back from her face. She opened her eyes slowly and looked up at me like a small hopeless child. "Mama, Mama, I'm sorry. Please understand. It isn't that I don't love you. It's just that I can't stay home from school. It would mean I wouldn't be able to go to college in the fall. I want to go. I want to find out about myself. Be on my own and learn how to be special in my own way. Maybe become a writer. Please, *please*, try to understand," I begged.

Her eyes were far away, but I could tell that she was listening. Slowly the misty vagueness that surrounded her face disappeared. There was a slight feeling of pressure on my palm. She was trying to squeeze it. Her face looked relaxed, almost relieved.

"I understand," she said simply, in a hoarse whisper. Incredibly, I knew that she did. My tears of relief spilled over onto her green blanket. She smiled a tiny smile at me and gently lifted her hand up to my face to touch it. Her fingers traced a miniature circle on my cheek and then dropped to

93

her lap. She drifted back to sleep. I looked at my sleeping mother and felt a sudden feeling of release—the way a hiker feels when she removes a heavy pack and moves lightly and freely without it.

Graduation was fast approaching. It seemed like all of a sudden the school was going mad with preparation. Caps and gowns had to be rented and fitted. Our classes were interrupted so that we could practice marching down the aisle.

I felt completely uncoordinated. March! *That* would have been easy. This was more of a slow dance—a two-step. Mrs. King demonstrated it in her best posture. Right foot forward. Left foot meets it. Pause. Left foot forward. Right foot meets it. Pause. It was those stupid pauses. The school auditorium was raked. It sloped downward at what felt like a ninety-degree angle. Every time we paused, I seemed to tip and fall forward, bumping the person in front of me. This, of course, set up a chain reaction, usually ending in a minor scuffle.

When they added the school band, the whole thing turned into instant chaos. That's when I began to enjoy myself. It was as if no one had ever graduated before. All the teachers stuck with the job of organizing us were at a loss as to how to do it.

Kids kept tripping as they went up the stairs to pretend to receive their diplomas. There were traffic jams, bottlenecks, and "entirely too much giggling." The whole business "lacked dignity."

The orchestra or band added a circus element as it squeaked out "Pomp and Circumstance." The accent was heavily on brass. It seemed that everyone played either trombone or trumpet. Flat or sharp. The string section—two or three valiant violinists and one cellist (not Carol)—fought hard to be heard above the din, but all I could hear of them was a high-pitched sawing noise.

We rehearsed and rehearsed with little improvement. Our teachers' only hope was that the reality of the actual graduation would sober us up and mold us into a dignified unit. I hoped it would all stay as chaotic and funny as it was then.

On prom night a bunch of my dateless friends got together at fat Carol's house to have our own private celebration. I was the only one there who could honestly say I'd turned down a date to the prom. Two weeks before, Bruce Bomes had called to ask me to go with him. But forgetting everything I had recently felt for him, I said no. For some crazy reason, I was still hung up on Bobby Gomez's good looks. It was now or never. I took a big gulp of air and called Bobby Gomez to ask him to "escort" me to the prom. Of course, he had already asked someone. I swallowed my enormous pride and called Bruce Bomes back to tell him that I'd changed my mind and how happy I'd be to go with him.

"Lisl," Bruce Bomes said miserably. "When you said no, I asked Patty Rappaport, and *she* said yes."

"Oh," was all I could say as I hung up the phone. My humiliation was supreme and, I realized, deserved. I was left without a date. The only consolation was that most of my favorite people were in the same boat. So, instead of mourning our collective fate, we decided to have a party.

Carol's parents made a vat of punch and lots of delicious fattening snacks. The rest of us brought our own contributions. It promised to be more fun than the prom. And anyway, it was so much nicer to spend prom night in jeans instead of dumb long dresses. Only Carol's mother seemed to be upset. She kept popping in, looking us over, and sadly wagging her head back and forth. I could tell she was thinking of her own prom ages ago and feeling sorry for all of us and especially for her daughter.

Jeff was there and even pimply Andrew Guth. And Jo, though she didn't go to our school and it wasn't her prom night, had been invited. Abby, who's always been an organizer, led us in a game of "Name That Tune," using Carol's parents' ancient records. It was silly but a lot of fun.

Andrew Guth turned out to be a secret romantic—he knew every old Frank Sinatra song by heart and won almost every time.

The winner got the chance to audition for an appearance on the Tonight Show—our version—as a singer. Poor shy Andrew won, and after an awful lot of protests he surprised us again by singing an aria from Carmen *in French!* The things you learn when it's almost too late!

We spent the rest of the night laughing and gossiping and planning an attack on the high school gymnasium. All of us in our sloppy clothes would escort each other to the prom with great ceremony, arriving at the perfect time to cause the greatest disturbance.

Jeff decided to rehearse his part. First he pulled his long blond hair into a neat ponytail behind his head; then he ran out the door. In two minutes he returned, took a deep bow, pinned a maple leaf on my T-shirt, and asked me for the honor of a dance. I curtsied and attempted a graceful pirouette. When I managed to unwind, I had fallen into Jo's lap, and Jeff lay sprawled on the living-room floor. He had tripped over Andrew's long legs.

For the next hour or so we put on some real music and took turns dancing with each other. Carol and Jeff were amazing together. They looked like a pair of disco superstars. Carol twirled and spun and never missed a beat. Jeff strutted like a rock star. We switched partners and did the Latin Hustle, the New York Hustle, and the Three Count Hustle—Jo's and my specialty. Then we all got together in a line and did the Bus Stop. Andrew Guth didn't know how to do it, but after a few false starts he was really good. I could feel the whole house and all the furniture rocking and vibrating in time to the music.

It was two o'clock in the morning when we finally split up—sweaty and achy and tired and very, very happy. I hadn't had so much fun in months.

The next day, I sat bleary-eyed on the edge of my mom's bed describing prom night. I thought a good account of our crazy antics might entertain her and make her smile. But when I looked up, I realized she wasn't listening.

"Mom, don't you want to know what we did?"

She didn't seem to hear me. In fact, she didn't seem to see me.

She was incredibly weak now. In the past few days it had become too much for her to ride up and down the stairs in our human chair. She spent every day in bed, lying on her back, sleeping when the painkillers permitted it. The rest of the time she lay staring at the ceiling, quietly moaning. Three times a day, against her increasingly strong protests, we held her up to feed her small amounts of chopped vegetables and fruits. She was no

98

longer interested in food, and, on this day, I realized, she was no longer interested in life.

"Mama," I pleaded. "*Please* listen to me."

She didn't answer. She didn't even blink. She was off in her own peculiar world—a world that centered on the ceiling. It was as if there was an invisible movie up there—visible only to her.

"What do you see?" I asked.

As if in answer, she moaned softly.

I sat on her bed feeling bewildered and helpless. I couldn't seem to get her attention. But then I heard her mumbling and muttering to herself, and despite the faintness of her voice, I could understand what she was saying.

"Mama. . . . Papa," she called.

But her mother and father had died long ago when she was only a little girl.

"Pansies," she called.

Pansies were her favorite flower.

Suddenly I knew what she was seeing on the ceiling. It was a story she loved to repeat. How when she was little, right after her parents died, she got very sick and had to stay in bed for many, many weeks. Her grandmother, who was very old at the time, bought her a window box full of brown and purple and yellow pansies. Every day she watched them watching her. Their velvety smiling faces were her only friends during her long illness.

I went berserk with the idea of buying her

some. Maybe I could tune her back into life. Why hadn't I thought of it sooner? I quietly excused myself, knowing that she'd make no response to my leaving, but still feeling the sting of being ignored. I ran to my bedroom, unrolled a sock, and took out some money. Then I raced to my parents' car, and drove a bit too fast to the nearest nursery.

When I returned, I was carrying a huge window box full of grinning pansies. My mother was still in that strange semiconscious state. I sat down on the bed, the window box in my lap, and gently called to her.

"Mama, look at me. See what I've brought you." No movement. "Mama, please look at me. I've brought you something." Still no movement. Not even any recognition that I had gone and returned. I took a deep breath and touched her bony arm.

Once in an art class, they'd had a skeleton named Gussie, and we had to draw it. It was very hard work and I hated doing it, but it had taught me the intricate structure that made us all human beings—equal under the flesh and fat we hide out in.

I'd done a mind game and won it with my mother. Whenever I looked at her body, I pretended it was that skeleton. For the last few weeks I had been able to see her bone joints clearly. As long as I remembered the art-class skeleton, it all seemed natural, and I could keep my feelings of fear and

100

repulsion to a minimum. After all, I was just seeing what we *all* looked like underneath our separate skins.

There was still a layer of skin covering her, but the fullness and curves were no longer there. I thought of fat Carol. Under all that fat was a skeleton similar in size and shape to the one in art class and to the one that was now so clearly my mother. I wondered how Carol would feel if she knew what I knew.

When I touched my mom, her eyes seemed to clear a bit and she turned her head ever so slightly in my direction.

"Mama." I tried again. "Look! Pansies!"

She twisted her head around towards me and looked at the tiny meadow of pansies. Then, without a word or sign, she turned away.

I felt a surge of sadness work its way through my body, and then I was crying. My mother was far away in her own private world, and I guessed that that world was far more important to her than pansies or me. I couldn't prevent the sound of sobs from leaving my lips. But it didn't matter. My mom was staring at the mysterious movie on the ceiling. I don't think she even heard me crying.

In typing class the next morning, I was still upset. We were completing our tests for the end of the course. Miss Molloy dictated business letter after business letter. It was our job to type them perfectly, sitting erect in our chairs, eyes riveted on the blackboard at the front of the room and not on the keys.

"Gentlemen: I wish to notify you that your letter of 21, December, concerning the estate of. . . ."

My mind wandered. I couldn't stop thinking of my mom. It was as if she had already died. I mean she was alive, breathing, even occasionally moving, but she didn't seem to care any more. For conversation, pansies, or me. For *life.*

What was it like to know you were dying? Was the answer on the ceiling? Was that why she spent so much time staring at it? It must be terrifying to know you'll never see a tree again. Never see the people you love. I'd kill myself. Pretty ironic. Kill myself, rather than die. But I would. How could anyone deal with the idea that they were about to die?

I remembered back when we all first met Sam, how my mom had said, "I don't feel as if I'm dying. I feel as if I'm getting better each day. Maybe I won't die." I remembered how, not so long ago, she'd played that impossible game. As if she could cheat death by asking us all to give up our lives and stay with her! It all seemed far away now. I knew she'd given up all her hopes and games.

"Your cooperation in this matter will be greatly appreciated. . . ."

That was it. What happened when you gave up hoping and struggling, when you knew you couldn't win? What did you do?

If it was me, I'd take a long look at everything I liked most in my life. Sort of a good-bye. That would mean my friends, my family, books, writing, flowers, trees. . . . Oh, I couldn't think of everything right off. But I'd also *do* a lot of things— swim, run, walk, lie on my back and look up at the sky. But then I realized, if I was as sick as my mom was, I couldn't do *any* of those things, so I'd just have to remember what it felt like to do them. That would really kill me. How could you think of all the beautiful things in life and know that you'd never be able to do them again? Never ever.

"We shall recall, with great affection and gratitude, the effort you have made on the part of our client. . . ."

The pansies. Of course. If she had tuned into them, the pain would have been unendurable. It was obvious. She loved them too much.

It was all a natural protective device. Your mind tuned out. Everything that was important in life had to become unimportant, meaningless. If you kept on caring, dying would be terrible. If you tuned out, it was easy. A quiet slow sinking into

103

silence and peace. Like a smooth slow slide, with eyes closed, into a warm waterhole. If you opened your eyes, you might see a beautiful tree or hear a friend calling to you, and then you'd realize how steep the slide actually was, how deep and dark the water. Then you'd be afraid. But the protective device saved you. It turned you inwards, away from life and the people and the things in it.

"Until that time, we shall forever remain with abiding affection,

Yours. . . "

She had turned away from me, too. She had tuned me out. Not just the pansies. I supposed that meant she cared. But my eyes filled with tears when I realized that my mother had to protect herself from me. It was far safer to rest her eyes and her mind on the ceiling rather than on her daughter. It was more comfortable when she wasn't being "entertained" and diverted by my prom-night stories and gifts of flowers. I felt empty. As if something had been ripped away. Something important like my arm or leg. It was as if I'd lost some essential part of myself.

"Lisl Gilbert! Eyes up! Staring at the keys. I'm afraid you've failed *this* one," barked Miss Molloy.

I looked up to find Miss Molloy's prim figure standing erect at the front of the classroom, arms crossed precisely at chest level, staring hawk-eyed at me. In an effort to keep the tears from spilling out, I'd lowered my eyelids, and I guess she thought I was peeking at the keys. I was too upset to protest and too weak to argue.

Before I knew what I was doing, I jumped up, grabbed my books, and ran out the door, leaving a trail of mutterings and concerned sounds behind me and one distinct. "Well, I never!" from the lips of sweet Miss Molloy. Never mind defending myself, I thought. Let someone else do it. I wasn't a cheater. You'd think Miss Molloy would know that by now and have the decency to ask what was wrong. Anyway, who cared? It was all so unimportant. My mother was dying. Actually dying.

And that very night the end unquestionably began. My mom was taken back to the hospital. And this time we knew it was for good. No more journeys up and down the steps. No more days spent in the bedroom staring at the ceiling. She gave us her final command.

We were all together—Jim and Jane, my dad and I—sitting around the bedroom, staring at my mom for hours. Except for her strange breathing and the squawk of some shiny black crows that had congregated outside our house, there was no sound. It was if we were *all* half dead. Then my mom started moaning and hoarsely calling, "I want to die. Let me die." It was a weak call. It was a desperate call. But it was also an undeniable command. "Let me die."

Like a bunch of foolish seals, we all jumped up and barked, "You don't mean that!" "Don't say that!" and "No, you can't." We spoke all at once, so that she couldn't possibly have heard any of us—even if she'd wanted to.

Then she tried painfully to sit up. My father and I gently pulled her up and held her steady, but it was as if something had buckled around her middle. She fell forward like a broken doll.

"She's collapsed," Jane screamed. "She's dead!" she gasped.

But she wasn't. As my father and I lifted her body back up and replaced it flat on the bed, we heard an almost inaudible sound. "Hos . . . Hos. . . ."

"Hospital," Jim translated. "Call the hospital, Jane. Get an ambulance." His words sounded firm and final. They were the ones I'd been dreading all these long months. The time had finally come.

It seemed like only a second later that two blond young men in white uniforms barged up the stairs into the bedroom carrying a metal stretcher. Like waiters, they cleared us all away and lifted my disjointed, broken-doll mother onto the hard metal stretcher. She rattled against it, bone against steel, as they whisked her down the steps and out the door.

I was terrified, but when last I saw her as they loaded her into the ambulance, she looked peaceful, calm, and contented. She'd gotten what she wanted.

We spent a long night in the emergency room, checking her in, waiting, pacing, and drinking up coffee along with sympathetic glances. I saw all kinds of sights—red-faced drunks brought in by pink-faced policemen, a man who kept punching a nurse until she finally wrestled him into submission, a woman all bloody from an auto accident. And in the background the moans of people we couldn't see, and the undeniable screams of my mother to whose wasted veins they were trying, without success, to attach an intravenous feeding device.

Hours later, she was wheeled up to a small room and attached to various tubes. They were going to give her transfusions. For what? I found myself wondering again. To prolong her life and her agony yet another day or two? They gave her a shot, and finally she was calm again and sleeping. They told us to go home and do the same. There was nothing to do but wait. It was "only a matter of time." A day, maybe two, maybe more. Certainly no more than a week, they assured us, as if we would be pleased at the news.

Every day after school I visited my mom. When the transfusions were completed, she was almost perky. For the first time in weeks, she occasionally said a few words or looked at me. We couldn't have conversations, but I knew she understood and was listening.

They were giving her drugs for pain and drugs to keep up her spirits, so the whole experience was really just a gift from the "miracle" of modern medicine. My mom was like a flattened inner tube with a hole in it that they kept inflating with new blood and drugs. As the drugs wore off or the infusions wore thin, she'd drift off into that stupor and become lost again in the world of the hospital ceiling. Then they'd reconnect the transfusion tubes, give her another shot, and she'd be back in the room with us.

After a while, we realized what torture we were putting her through—inflating her only to watch her inevitably deflate. We told the doctors we wanted no more artificial stimuli—no more mechanical prolonging of her life. "Just let nature take its course," we said. It was easy to say then. She had just had another transfusion and was recognizably alive.

Graduation was a few days away, and I had decided not to go. Everyone else disagreed and said so in front of my mom, who weakly nodded her head to indicate that she, too, wanted me to go. So I agreed. But it seemed irrelevant in the face of what was going on. Besides, quite frankly, I was afraid my mom would die before graduation, or worse, during it. I had this eerie feeling that the moment I received my diploma, she'd collapse and die.

We had two days off before the special day, and I spent them with my mom. Thanks to Abby, who was in my typing class, Miss Molloy had forgiven my trespasses. Abby had explained my "troubles" and Miss Molloy had discounted that one test, admitting that my work, until that day, had been "excellent." So I spent the two days in a kind of limbo—waiting to go through both the ceremony of graduation and the ritual of death.

My mother was fading so quickly now, it was a little frightening to be alone with her. It seemed like she might die any moment. Her breathing was almost impossible to hear, and she was far, far away in that strange land. I sat in her room reading a book, shuffling through magazines from the hospital's waiting room, and gazing at my mom, trying to memorize her face. It was a far cry from the one I used to know, but I recognized it, and as long as the sheet that covered her kept rising and falling, I felt some comfort.

It was odd. I felt two completely opposing feelings. I dreaded the thought of my mom dying, but I also couldn't bear another moment of this waiting. I found myself wishing she would hurry up and die. The doctor had said "a week at the most" and a week was already up. To look at her, it seemed impossible that she could last another second. Yet several days ago, we'd all thought her time was up, and today she was still breathing.

The burden of watching through the days and waiting through the nights for the inevitable telephone call from the hospital was getting to all of us. We were exhausted, on edge, unhappy, and at the same time impatient. When would it ever end?

My dad had come to the hospital to watch for a time, while Jim and Jane went about the task of selecting a casket at a local funeral parlor. For once, I was glad to be considered the baby. It all seemed a little indecent. My mom wasn't even dead, but as Jim said, we'd known for months and it was about time we faced the unpleasant realities. The day before, my dad and I had chosen a burial spot in the cemetery. So everything was in order. All we needed was the guest list for the funeral and, last but not least, my mother's death.

But my mother was hanging on with that same perverse tenacity that had kept her running all through her life. It hardly seemed possible that she was alive, yet she continued to live as if she still had some further business to do.

While I was sitting by her bedside feeling the conflicting tugs of wanting her to live and wanting her to die, she suddenly made a peculiar sound— her first sound in days. My dad was sitting

110

slumped in the extra chair a nurse had provided, and he looked as shocked and frightened as I felt. We stood on opposite sides of her bed staring at her. She was trying to say something, but she couldn't do it. Days before, they had stopped feeding her through the IV, and she was very close to death. Her lips were parched and she was incredibly weak.

"What is it, Mom?" I asked, my voice cracking with fear.

"*Echh. Rrrr,*" she tried, and then she managed a small sigh. She couldn't speak, so my father and I played Twenty Questions.

"Is it about the children?" my father asked, his knuckles white from grasping the bed rungs so tightly. No answer. More sounds.

"Do you need anything?" I asked, thinking as soon as I spoke how stupid that question was. She couldn't possibly answer it.

"*Echh. Rrrr,*" she said, straining to get the words out. Her forehead knitted up in frustration. We were striking out. We asked question after question after question with no success. It was obvious that she was trying to tell us something. Suddenly I realized what it was. Through the meaningless, helpless sounds, the horror of cancer and death, and all the misunderstandings of a lifetime, I finally crashed through the communications barrier.

"It's all right, Mom. I understand," I said. My

father looked at me as if I was crazy. "You know that we love you, don't you? That we've always loved you. And we know that you love us. That you'll always love us."

My mother's forehead relaxed. The strange awful sound subsided. Then a most amazing thing happened. She lifted both of her hands as if to reach us. My father grabbed one, and I the other. We held her tightly as she pressed our hands as hard as she could. I may have imagined it, but I think she smiled. My father's lips trembled, and his face moved in several directions. A tear crept slowly down his left cheek.

How strange life was! All my life I'd never been sure that my mom knew I loved her. All their married life my father had had the same problem. I figured we'd never know for sure if that tiny smile meant she'd finally understood. But at least I knew she was really trying to understand. For the first time in her life she had slowed down enough to listen. And it had taken cancer to do it. It was all terribly sad and ironic.

I remembered my speech to Sam about finding and doing a few things I really enjoyed, instead of running so fast I couldn't see or appreciate what I was running past. I vowed I'd always keep my eyes open to see what and who was around me. Otherwise, I might miss out, the way my mom had, on some of the people who loved me.

My dad decided to stay another hour or so and

112

wait for Jim and Jane to return, but I'd had it. I was tired, and filled with all kinds of strange emotions: relief that I'd finally communicated with my mom, fear that she would soon die, dread that the ordeal of waiting would go on even a minute longer, sadness, and a feeling of loss, as if she'd already died. Thoughts spun around and around in my head like a crazy carousel.

Mom the superstar had died long ago. She was now only a distant memory. There was virtually nothing left that resembled my mom except the thin shell that was still her body. I felt an empty sadness that I thought must be what people call mourning. That was it, I was mourning my mother's death even though it hadn't happened yet.

As I slowly left the room and entered the long green hospital corridor, I passed the waiting room and saw a familiar face. It was Sam.

"Hi," she whispered. "Come sit and talk to me for a minute. Okay?" She led me into the yellow waiting room with its orange plastic couches and ugly floral pictures. "I've been calling the hospital to find out about Jean's condition. It's any minute now, isn't it?" I nodded. Sam reached out and touched my arm. "How are you?"

"Okay. Confused. It's as if she was already dead. Only she isn't, and I wish she was, but I also wish she wouldn't. Do you understand?"

"Yes, I do. Technically speaking, she's still

alive, but the energy and spirit that was your mom is leaving. Perhaps it's already gone. So, in a sense, she *has* already died."

"Where does it go? All that energy?"

"I don't know for sure. No one does. But I do know that it can be passed on through the people she's touched. Like you. You can choose the things you like best about your mother's spirit and personality and keep them. Perhaps one day you can pass them on to your own children. Right now, to other people. You can discard some things and keep what you want." She touched my cheek.

"Sort of like weeding a garden," I whispered. "You remove the things you don't like, so they don't strangle the things you want to let grow."

"Yes, that's it. After your mother is dead, you'll still have her energy and all that creative ability to choose from. You already have it, and I think you've learned to recognize it."

I knew Sam was right as usual. I couldn't hide from myself anymore. I knew I wanted to be a writer—to study writing and literature in college next year. (Jim would certainly be pleased.) And it was comforting to know that the energy for the work and the life that was ahead of me came in part from my mom. That way, it felt like she'd always be with me, in a good way.

"Well, I'm glad we were able to talk," Sam whispered. "Have a good time at graduation. It's tomorrow, isn't it?"

114

The back pocket of my jeans felt especially heavy. I still had my two guest tickets for graduation in it. Since no one from my family could come, I'd invited Jo, but I'd decided to give the other ticket away. All of a sudden, I found myself yanking one out and offering it to Sam. I felt silly and shy. "Would you like to come? My friend Jo will be there, and if you could, I'd love for you to come."

Sam reached for the ticket and grinned. "I thought you'd never ask." Suddenly I felt an unfamiliar feeling—my face was crinkling and I was smiling. Sam and I gave each other a huge bear hug. With Jo and Sam coming, it felt as if my family would be there after all—my family of friends.

That night, as we had done the long week through, we all slept close to the phones, expecting them to ring, hoping they would, fearing they would. Somehow we finally fell asleep and awoke to discover that yet another night had gone by and, impossibly, my mother was still alive.

The four of us—Jim, Jane, my dad, and I—ate breakfast together. Jane gave me a "graduation kiss," and my father slapped me on the back and mumbled something about being proud. Then they all stumbled wearily out the door to go to the hospital, and left me to prepare for graduation.

I washed and dried my hair, cursing myself for letting it grow so long. It took almost an hour to dry and brush that giant mane into smooth soft waves of hair. But when finally it was done, I had to admit I didn't look bad. In honor of the special day I reddened my cheeks and added a bit of eye makeup and some lip gloss. Thin as I'd become, I looked older, and, I thought, more sophisticated.

I put on a plain white dress to wear under my graduation gown. Then I lifted the white robe from its box marked "Peerless Rental Wear." It was at least two sizes too large and a foot too long. When I put it on, I looked like Father Time. Someone had obviously sent me the wrong box, and now it was too late to do anything about it. The *pièce de résistance* was the cap which made me look like a small mouse wearing a huge record album on its head. My mood swung from high to low in a matter of seconds. I looked horrible and I felt terrible. The white shoes that completed the outfit pinched my toes and heels. Torture! Death by graduation.

Jo honked the horn of her parents' new car, and since there was nothing I could do to fix things, I dashed out the door.

"Now, shut up . . . ," I warned her, but it was too late. She'd already started.

"Hey . . . Well . . . if it isn't the Ghost of Christmas Past! Your Honor, may I present the distinguished . . . "

"Rat fink," I yelled. "Stop it! Just wait until

116

you graduate. I'm coming with a fleet of photographers. I'm warning you—can it, or you're in deep trouble."

"Okay, sweets. I got the message. And if it's any comfort, everyone else is going to look just as . . . good." She smiled wickedly.

When we got to the high school, Jo dropped me off to look for a place to park and to find her seat for the ceremony. She knew she'd be sitting next to Sam, and she seemed to be looking forward to it.

Inside, school was the way I loved it best. Complete chaos. Everywhere you looked, kids were milling about. With the boys in black gowns and the girls in white, we looked like a sea of penguins. Jo was right. I was positively glamorous compared to some of the others. We were all equally embarrassed, and everyone adjusted their caps in various directions in order to improve their looks. Abby wore hers at a jaunty angle like a French beret. Jeff tilted his forward over his nose like a baseball cap. Bruce Bomes looked as if he was doing military maneuvers as he moved his cap back and forth, desperately trying to keep it from accentuating his oversized ears. The only exception was Bobby Gomez who stood at the head of the line looking stunning as usual. For the rest of us, it was hopeless.

The teachers called us to attention, and miraculously we formed a line to be inspected before the procession began. A hidden voice called

117

out, "And they told me the army would be tough!" Everyone tittered until our drill sergeants commanded us to adjust our caps so that they fitted squarely on our heads. There was to be no variation in the way they were worn, so in the end we all looked equally ridiculous.

The orchestra struck up the first sharp notes of "Pomp and Circumstance" and we started the slow step-pause, step-pause march to our seats.

Amazingly, we all made it down the center aisle without mishap. There we neatly split into two equal parts—one that marched left, the other right. The problem arose when the time came to sit down. We'd been instructed to remain standing by our seats until the last graduate had filed in. Then, at precisely the same moment, we were to sit. It was all part of the dramatic effect Mrs. King had choreographed long ago for graduations.

Unfortunately, without turning around, it was nearly impossible to detect when the last kids had made it to their seats. Everyone sneaked a glance over their shoulders. When Gloria Zauderer finally took her place, we all felt paralyzed. Who dared to be the first to sit down and lead the others? I listened as hard as I could, but I couldn't hear a cue from our sergeants. They seemed as confused as we were.

The orchestra was starting its seventh squeaking chorus of "Pomp and Circumstance" when I saw the people in the front row sit down. By then, my feet were killing me, so I joined them. Soon mortar boards were bobbing up and down as everyone sat down whenever the spirit moved them. The effect was not as intended. We looked like corks bouncing in the water on a windy day.

Out came Mr. Donahue who gave a short speech and introduced Mr. Visco, the principal. He was gray-haired and wore a gray suit and old wire glasses, the kind you peel off your face. He loved doing that. It was for him, a form of punctuation. Whenever he said anything that was important and needed underlining, he'd peel off his glasses, lean forward on the lectern, and look us all in the eyes. A neat trick considering there were over six hundred of us.

His talk was full of ocean metaphors about "embarking on the ship of life," watching out for "the rough seas ahead," and "searching for that home port." Again, I could imagine Mittleman's voice yelling, "Trite. Hackneyed." But I knew he wouldn't dare criticize our leader, Mr. Visco.

It was time for the special awards. Andrew Guth won the science award. He really was brilliant. Good at science *and* English, not to mention singing. Someone named Sylvia Jones won the math award. Carol won the music award— a check for five hundred dollars "to help further her musical career"! And *I* won the English award!

When I heard my name called, I jumped to my feet and nearly raced to the stage. I couldn't believe it. But I remembered the Voice of Freedom Contest and slowed down to a sedate pace. When I reached Mr. Visco, he handed me a collection of Shakespeare's plays and a beautifully bound book of blank paper for writing. He shook my hand and congratulated me, and I got all teary. I was so excited. I wanted to kiss that tired gray man. Of course, I managed to resist the urge, thanked him, and returned to my seat, beaming like a huge light bulb.

I didn't even hear the rest of the awards, and before I knew it, I was back up on the stage to receive my diploma—a long piece of paper tied in purple cord.

Afterward, everyone crowded outside the high school. Jo and Sam made a sandwich out of me— one on one side, the other on the other, hugging me. They were as excited as I was, and it felt terrific to share my happiness with both of them.

All kinds of people came up to shake my hand or kiss me: my friends, kids I didn't know, and some parents who seemed to know me, though I had no idea who they were. Carol and I shook hands, and I whispered, "I told you you'd make it."

"Thanks," she blushed and smiled, all teary-eyed.

In the middle of the crowd, Bruce Bomes appeared and gave me a long kiss and an even longer look. "Hey, kiddo, congratulations."

120

"Thanks," I said, feeling a strange tingly sensation run through my body.

"Sorry we missed each other for the prom, but there's always this summer—if you'll condescend to go out with me."

"I'd like that," I said, suddenly feeling shy.

"Okay, I'll call you soon," he yelled, escaping into the crowd. When I turned around, Jo and Sam winked at me. Now I knew why I liked Sam— she was as devilish as Jo.

All the noise and laughter was exciting, but then I remembered it was time to go back to the hospital. There were parties that night that I hadn't told my family about for fear they'd make me go. I thanked Sam for coming, and hugged her. As she hurried off to catch a bus to work, I felt sad and lost. Jo must have noticed the expression on my face because she said, "Hey, you'll see her again. She likes you as much as I do." I smiled at Jo. We still had terrific "Rappaport."

We left the noisy crowd and walked to Jo's car in silence. When she dropped me off at the hospital, it was with some reassuring words, "Hey kid. Don't forget, I'm with you. It'll be okay." She jammed her foot on the accelerator and sped away as I turned toward the tall gray building.

I hurried into the elevator, got out and walked

slowly down the corridor, carrying the writing book and the diploma in one hand and the Shakespeare collection in the other. It wasn't hard to change from the euphoric mood that marked graduation to the somber one that greeted death.

I could hear my shoes clickety-clacking down the shiny floor like gunshots. My mom's corridor was the quietest one in the hospital. It was like death row at San Quentin. Everything was still. Everyone who stayed in the small rooms and everyone who visited them was just marking time.

I opened the door to my mom's room. My whole family was assembled around her bed. My father sat in one chair, crumpled up like a wrinkled prune, holding his head in his hands. Jane was in the other chair, quietly sobbing, while Jim, looking tense, rubbed her back.

The body in the bed, my mom, was barely alive and was certainly unaware of the tableau in front of her. I put down my books, stood by her bedside, and watched. Her body was working overtime to keep on going. Her breathing was excruciatingly loud and rasping, and it came with hardly any rhythm or regularity.

The whole thing was like a suspense film—a cliff-hanger. She'd breathe; there would be a long pause; and then we'd have to contend with the inevitable question of whether that awful rasping sound would ever be heard again. In our separate ways, we were all praying, wishing, counting, and

122

magicking for her. I had my fingers crossed on both hands. After what seemed like forever, it would come—a gasp of breath that sounded like someone drowning. Then silence again. Jim stared at me for a long time, looked at Jane and at my father, who seemed overcome, and said, "Why don't you go down to the cafeteria and get us something to drink?"

"What do you want?" I looked at my father. He just waved his hand vaguely in the air. I guessed that meant anything, although it might have meant nothing.

Jane said, "It doesn't matter. Just go."

Bossy, I thought, but I turned and left the room. I hurried to the elevator and down to the cheery cafeteria I had grown to detest. It was crowded with depressed families waiting to hear the results of operations and young doctors discussing "a superbly executed appendectomy" and "a clean—really clean—amputation." They sounded like sculptors working in stone. Listening to them made me feel nauseated and furious, both at the same time. Their laughter pierced my stomach and tempted me to scream, Shut up. Can't you remember that people are people and not merely bodies? But I kept my mouth shut. After all, they were wearing white coats and looked young, handsome, and knowledgeable. I figured I must be supersensitive and crazy.

I ordered four iced coffees and slowly carried

them upstairs in a cardboard carton that was soon soaking wet from all the bumps and narrow escapes I had with people in the cafeteria, the elevator, and the corridors.

When I came round the corner to our hallway, my heart began fluttering, and I saw speckled, flashing lights in front of my eyes. I began to sink to the floor to keep from fainting, but halfway down I remembered the carton of iced coffees. I pulled myself up and hurried toward the door to my mom's room. Outside, my family and two nurses were congregated. Jane was nearly hysterical, Jim was supporting her while tears ran down his red face, and my father was choking and snorting into a handkerchief while a nurse held his arm.

It had happened. After all these months, it was almost impossible to believe. I felt strangely numb. I could vaguely see a young nurse approach me. She took the carton from my hands and held me around the waist.

"Five minutes ago, at four fifty, your mother passed away."

"Passed away? You mean she's *dead*, don't you?!" I said angrily. What was this euphemistic junk? "I want to see her," I snapped and pushed the nurse aside and burst through my family, through the door. She followed me inside.

"Are you sure you'll be all right?" she asked gently, and suddenly I realized that she was concerned about me.

124

"Yes, I'm fine," I said, and turned to her to smile and prove it.

"Okay, I'll be outside if you need me." She quietly closed the door and left me alone with my dead mother. It was strange. She looked almost exactly the same as she had before I went down to the cafeteria: maybe a little paler and a bit yellowish, certainly more peaceful, but the same. She was in exactly the same position in which I had left her. Her right hand still up near her face where I guess, unconsciously, she thought it would help her to breathe. I couldn't believe she was dead. She looked more tranquil than she'd looked when she was alive.

I remembered that business about people's hearts sometimes stopping and how doctors brought them back to life by heart massage. Some of those people had said they'd been vaguely conscious of things in the living world, even though they'd been legally and medically dead. I knew absolutely nothing could bring my mom back to life, but I wondered if maybe enough of that energy Sam had mentioned was still in the room for her to hear me, so I sat down in the chair next to her bed and talked to her.

"I hope you can hear me, Mama. I just want to say a few things before you go away. I know I've told you all this before, but . . . well, I wanted to tell you . . . one last time . . . I love you. I always will. I guess in a lot of ways we never really understood each other all that well. But I've learned a lot about myself recently, and I guess I've grown up some. I wish you could have stayed around longer so we could have gotten to know each other better . . . as adults. You know . . . woman to woman. Maybe in some ways we'll still be together. Maybe in a better way than before. I hope so. I'm going to miss you, Mama. An awful lot. Please miss me a little."

I was crying, crying the saddest and deepest tears I had ever cried. But in a strange way, I felt better. As if I'd been cleaned out. I looked at my dead mother lying so still in her bed, and suddenly I had an overwhelming urge to touch her and kiss her good-bye. It seemed perverse, but when I looked at her, I realized it wasn't. My mom's spirit might be gone, but her body, the house it had lived in, was still there. Thin and broken down as it was, I still loved it. I stood up and moved closer to the side of her bed. I took her left hand and pressed it against my cheek and kissed it. A warm tear rolled down my cheek onto her cold hand.

I backed away to take a final look and memorize her face for the last time, when slowly, the way an autumn leaf detaches itself from a tree and floats quietly down to the ground, her right hand softly left her cheek and drifted down alongside her body onto the bed linen.

I jumped a little. It was as if she was alive. A voice behind me said gently, "Don't be afraid. That happens sometimes a short time after death. She's dead." And the nurse who'd been silently keeping watch over me took me by the hand and guided me out the door away from my mother forever.

The doctor was waiting in the hall to issue the death certificate, and my family—what was left of it—looked like a human chain of mourners. They had all linked arms and were waiting for me. We left together, but I walked alone. I needed to feel my body moving by itself. It seemed miraculous that my mother was dead and I could still walk. One foot went out, then the other, and I moved forward. Or I stopped. It was incredible.

We left the hospital, and I noticed the carefully trimmed emerald-green grass that met the gray-paved paths to and from the hospital. The green was so bright and new and fresh, and the gray was so dull and dead. It was like life meeting death. I purposely violated the hospital rules and walked on the grass. "To walk through fields on a summer's day." Well, it wasn't exactly fields. But it was almost summer.

Soon it would be fall, and I would start college; and the green I'd be walking on would be the green of a campus. That's when I'd find out for sure if I was what my mom had called special.

I clutched the Shakespeare collection, the writing book, and the diploma in my hands, knowing that I'd already begun to find out. I loved my friends and family, but there were times like now, when I needed to be alone to think. I liked to read, to write, to say what was on my mind. Sam had helped me. *I* had helped me. I felt much older. If I was honest with myself, I had to admit that I was beginning to feel unique, maybe even a little special. But somehow, on this day, that knowledge only made me sadder. I wanted my mom to be around to see me grow.

It was sad to think that my father would be all alone when I left for school. Jim and Jane would be going back to New York after the funeral, and in only a few months I'd be leaving home, too. I hoped that by then my dad would have found a new job and a way to be happy. Maybe during the summer, we'd have a chance to get to know each other better. We'd never really tried before. I guessed that all of us—my dad, Jane, Jim, and I had a lot of things to figure out. A lot of new things to try. A lot of new things to do. But as I walked alone through the bright green grass away from the hospital, away from my mom, I felt a new kind of energy. I knew I'd make it. It was only a matter of time.

115298

DATE DUE

J
S   115298

AUTHOR
Schotter, Roni

TITLE
A matter of time.

DATE DUE	BORROWER'S NAME	ROOM NUMBER
RETURNED		
03 13 2	BAMBER MONICA	

J
S
Schotter, Roni
A matter of time.

Ohio Dominican College Library
1216 Sunbury Road
Columbus, Ohio 43219

DEMCO